"Am I so hard to remember?"

Not as hard as you are to forget. The
thought sprang from nowhere, and
as much as Alex hated the truth of it,
it was undeniable.

He hadn't forgotten, either. But the way
he looked at her now told her he was
remembering different things—like the
way she'd turned her back on him.
The way she'd left him cold.

He was a different person from that
boy she'd met so long ago. Well, she'd
changed, too. She was older, wiser, a
mother. The mother of his son!

*Trish Morey is a hot new Australian
author! Harlequin Presents® is proud to
present Trish's passionate and provocative
debut novel THE GREEK BOSS'S DEMAND*

Trish Morey

THE GREEK BOSS'S DEMAND

GREEK TYCOONS

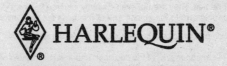

HARLEQUIN®

TORONTO • NEW YORK • LONDON
AMSTERDAM • PARIS • SYDNEY • HAMBURG
STOCKHOLM • ATHENS • TOKYO • MILAN • MADRID
PRAGUE • WARSAW • BUDAPEST • AUCKLAND

For Gavin, who always believed.
And for Jane, who helped make it possible.
Thanks, guys

ISBN 0-373-12444-9

THE GREEK BOSS'S DEMAND

First North American Publication 2005.

www.eHarlequin.com

Printed in U.S.A.

CHAPTER ONE

A PROPERTY company!

What was Nick Santos supposed to do with a half-share in a property company all the way over here in Australia? Especially one that by rights should have gone in its entirety to his cousin Sofia.

Taking note of the flashing light over his head, Nick duly fastened his seat belt for the descent into Sydney.

He'd never thought of his uncle Aristos as having a sense of humour, but he had to have been joking to come up with this scheme.

Half the company on condition that he stay and head up the business for six months, teaching Sofia whatever she needed to know to run the business herself.

It was crystal-clear what his late uncle had intended by his strange bequest. Nick was no stranger to the practice of arranged marriages, and he wasn't about to have one foisted on him.

As soon as he'd paid his respects to Sofia he'd gift her the balance of the company by leaving Australia and forfeiting his share of the inheritance. He didn't need the hassle when there were more important issues to consider at home—even if he had left the business in the safe hands of Dimitri, his second in charge.

He settled back into his seat, taking in the view as the plane came in for landing.

So this was Sydney. He caught a glimpse of the Sydney Harbour Bridge, with the Opera House nestled alongside—architectural icons of the busy harbour—before city buildings swallowed up the view and he had to content himself with watching the endless procession of red roofs and blue backyard pools skating under the plane as it descended steadily towards the airport.

In spite of the disruption to his schedules he could almost thank Aristos for finally getting him here. He'd grown up hearing tales of fortunes to be made in the new world. His mother's brother had made a success of it, that much was sure.

And he'd met a few Australians in his time. One in particular stuck in his mind—a girl he'd met on the island of Crete. Years ago now.

She'd been all pale skin and freckles, with long blonde hair and smiling blue eyes that infected you with laughter. Together they'd explored the crumbling ruins that dotted the island, and her fascination and boundless enthusiasm over the remnants of a civilisation so ancient had been contagious. She'd made him feel guilty that even as a student of archaeology he tended to take his country's rich history for granted. Yet at the same time she'd also made him feel proud to be Greek. She had been beautiful, vibrant and spirited—and, as it turned out, fickle.

He exhaled a long breath he hadn't realised he'd been holding and stretched back travel-weary shoulders into the wide first-class seat.

The plane touched down and taxied to the terminal, finally pulling to a halt. Everyone around him was stirring, impatient from the long flight and eager to clear Customs in the least amount of time. A smiling flight attendant appeared at his arm with his jacket.

He nodded his thanks and forced his mind back to the present.

That spring was a long time ago, and right now he had more pressing problems to think about. His place was not here. He belonged back in Greece. And as soon as he had sorted out this unusual bequest that was exactly where he was headed.

CHAPTER TWO

ALEX opened the office door and slammed into her past.

Nick Santos!

She had to be dreaming. Nick was back home in Athens, running the family engineering empire. He had no business here in Sydney, standing in the foyer of the Xenophon Property Group.

Especially not today, with the office reopening after Aristos's heart attack and funeral, when she was already days behind in getting out the monthly rental invoices, and with the new boss—some far-flung relative—expected at any time.

Not today? Who was she kidding? Not ever.

But it couldn't be Nick.

She blinked, but when she opened her eyes he was still there.

And it was still Nick.

Strange how there was no way she could mistake him—how she could be so absolutely positive, even after all this time. Even though he was standing there with his back to her, talking to Sofia, still she knew it was him—sensed it was him—with just a glimpse of profile and the wave of thick, dark hair licking at the collar of his oh-so-white shirt. Knew it from his

stance, manly and confident. Knew it in the message
her heart was suddenly beating.

Adrenalin danced with her pulse, readying her for
fight or flight. *No contest.* There was no way her feet
would move forward. Not even the welcoming scent
of the coffee machine's fresh brew could beckon her
inside. She would back out right now, quickly, and
he would never see her. Maybe by the time she came
back he'd be gone, back out of her life, back into her
past where he belonged.

She let her arm go slack on the door, letting it fall
back towards her. Maybe, if she was quiet...

'There you are,' Sofia called, stepping out from behind his shoulder, looking every part the grieving
daughter in her black silk skirt suit, her dark hair tied
back into a sleek, high ponytail. And before she'd had
a chance to respond he'd spun around, arresting her
retreat with the sheer impact of his features so that
the only movement she was capable of was the in-
voluntary quiver that descended her spine. His dark
eyes narrowed, his gaze sweeping her from top to toe
before settling on her face. Then his nostrils flared as
his lips curved ever so slightly.

'So it is you,' he stated, his chin kicking up a notch.

She swallowed hard. In the eight-plus years since
she'd seen Nick she'd often imagined what their first
words would be and how he would say them if ever
they met again. Not once had she imagined Nick
would coldly and dispassionately come out with
something like, *'So it is you.'*

'Who were you expecting?' she said, finally convincing her muscles there was no way out of it but to push open the door and enter the lobby. 'Kylie Minogue?'

She winced inwardly at the harshness of her words. *Damn, but how were you supposed to think in situations like this?*

'Alex?' Sofia turned from one to the other, confusion apparent on her face. 'I want to introduce you to my cousin, Nick Santos, who arrived yesterday. But…am I missing something here?'

She couldn't talk. Her throat too tight, her mouth ashen. And all the while Nick just kept on watching her intently, until she felt pinned down in the accusing gaze of his bottomless dark eyes. He had a score to settle with her; that much his hard-edged glare made clear. Aside from that, he was obviously as unimpressed at seeing her as she was stunned at seeing him.

It was Nick who finally broke the impasse.

'Alexandra and I have met before. Haven't we?'

Under his continuing scrutiny the laptop in her hand suddenly felt unbearably heavy, threatening to slip from her damp palm. She screwed her fingers tighter around the handle till her fingernails dug painfully but reassuringly into her skin. That was her laptop taken care of. Now she just had to focus on making sure her knees held up.

'I guess so,' she managed at last. 'At least I'm pretty sure we have. It was such a long time ago.'

A muscle twitched in Nick's cheek.

'Am I so hard to remember?'

Not as hard as you are to forget. The thought sprang from nowhere and, as much as Alex hated the truth of it, it was undeniable. Long nights alone, remembering their shared time back on Crete and wishing things could have turned out differently, were testament to that.

He hadn't forgotten either. But the way he looked at her now told her he was remembering different things—like the way she'd turned her back on him. The way she'd left him cold.

She took a deep breath, but Sofia was too impatient to wait for her response in a conversation that was obviously far too personal for her liking.

'Spill the beans, you two. So how do you know each other?'

Nick's eyes bored into Alex. The cold heat of them was like a kick in the gut.

'How about it? Or are you having trouble remembering that too?'

She raised her chin a fraction and shifted her gaze to Sofia. Her brain was still in shock at seeing Nick after all this time, and it was much easier trying to think while she wasn't looking directly at him. Where the damning questions in his eyes couldn't reach her.

And she had to think. Had to calm down. Sofia was still raw from the shocking death of her father. Even under the mask of her professionally applied make-up the shadows and puffiness around her eyes were all too evident. Sofia certainly didn't need Alex's baggage on top of her own.

'Crete. About—' She stopped and licked her lips. *No need to be too specific.* 'Some years ago. I was on holiday with my family. Nick was working in his university break on an archaeological dig. We met at the palace of Minos.'

'Cool,' said Sofia, although Alex noted the word she'd used mirrored her tone. Sofia was obviously less than impressed. 'So, did you know he was related to Aristos?'

'No, I had no ide—'

A cold ooze of dread rolled over her. *God, no!* Not *that* relative of Aristos? Not the one who was taking over the company?

'Way cool! Then I hardly have to introduce you to each other. That's going to make it easier, with you guys working together.'

Alex couldn't think of anything less cool as her world tilted and spun. When the direct line in her office rang, it was all she could do not to run and answer it.

'Excuse me,' she said instead, adding, 'I'm expecting this call. We'll have to catch up later.' Then she moved as quickly as she could while desperately trying to keep her balance on a planet that was shifting further off axis with every step.

She shut the door, plonked her laptop on the desk

and somehow dealt with the phone call while all the time her brain was registering only two words. Nick—*here*!

One hour later, Alex was still staring at the walls, the screensaver on her laptop the only sign of life in the room. How long she could stay secreted away in her office, she didn't know—but she'd do whatever it took to have as little to do with Nick Santos as possible, and until she had some sort of plan she didn't want to go anywhere near him.

It was weird, seeing him after so many years. Strange how they'd both thought themselves so grown up back then. He had seemed so strong and so much a man. At twenty-one he'd been more worldly and experienced than her. Yet now she could see how young they'd been. For it was obvious that the boy had become a man.

He looked every part the professional businessman. Gone was the long fringe that he'd used to flick out of his eyes with the toss of his head, replaced by a short, slick style. His dark features, even back then resonant with hidden depths, now seemed to sit more comfortably in a more mature face. Even his shoulders seemed broader.

He was a different person, clearly, from that boy she'd met so long ago.

Well, she'd changed too.

She was older, wiser, a mother.

The mother of his son!

Something like a garbled cry escaped from her lips.
Jason!

How in heaven's name was she going to prevent
him from finding out about Jason?

CHAPTER THREE

A BRIEF knock on her door made her look up, only to find Nick filling the space where the door had been.

She swallowed.

'What do you want?'

Nick took a step into her office, eyebrows raised.

'Is that any way to greet an old friend? It's not as if we're strangers after all.'

'It was a long time ago. You almost feel like a stranger.'

He hesitated. Tilted his head to one side.

'You have no idea how I feel, Alexandra.'

His words, and the flat way in which he delivered them, made her swallow. But that was nothing to how she felt when he moved closer to the desk. Panic pooled in her every cell.

Then he suddenly turned. For just a second Alex felt relief, but only for a second. She heard Nick mutter, 'Just wait—I'll be with you soon,' before closing the door. Alex caught a flash of black as Sofia, looking indignant, rushed by, then it swung shut and Nick wheeled and moved back across the office until he was standing just across the desk from her.

And then he was looking down at her—dark,

threatening and dangerous—and all Alex could think about was the pressure bearing down on top of her.

The pressure of being confronted by this man, her first love—*her first lover*—the pressure of knowing he was part of Aristos's world and had never been a real part of hers—the pressure of knowing the secret that lay between them like a chasm.

The chair-back pressed into her as she attempted, however fractionally, to increase the distance between them.

'Alexandra—'

She squeezed her eyes shut. The way he still said her name, just as he had back then, squeezing out the syllables till they seemed to curl in his rich, Mediterranean accent. Nobody had ever said her name like Nick had those weeks in Crete. It had made her feel sexy back then.

Only now she couldn't let it affect her. She was all grown up and things like that were the stuff of teenagers and holidays and holding hands. She was over it.

'Alexandra.'

She sucked in a breath, opened her eyes and forced what she hoped would pass as a businesslike expression onto her face.

'I guess you'll need to check the accounts, find out how the company is going. Our tax position—all that stuff.'

He blinked slowly. 'There's time for that later.'

'Good,' Alex said, a little too fast. 'I'm kind of

busy at the moment...' She shuffled a few papers on her desk for effect. 'Maybe I could drop the accounts into you later? I imagine you want to get things sorted out here and head back to Greece as soon as you can.'

Nick's eyes narrowed as he propped himself down on the edge of her desk and leaned dangerously close to her.

'I can see you're in the middle of something very important,' he whispered conspiratorially, nodding towards the computer. She followed his gesture and felt her cheeks heat till she was sure they matched the colour of the rosy-coloured pipe powering a cubic path around her computer screen.

Her hand reached out on impulse, but she snatched it back short of the keyboard. Better the screensaver right now than her desktop. Not with a photograph of Jason beaming out from it.

She looked up at him and grabbed a breath, anxious to steer the conversation to safe territory—wherever that might be.

'I was thinking...'

Both his eyebrows went up this time and he leaned over to swipe a pen from right in front of her, getting so close as to fill her senses with the subtle scent of his cologne overlaying the unmistakable essence of man. For a second it took her breath away, her line of thought erased, and she had no choice but to sit and watch as he began to tap the pen against the fingers of his other hand.

'Very reassuring to hear my uncle employed people

who can think.' He looked around, assessing the pale honey-coloured walls, the bookshelves and filing cabinets, as if taking an inventory. 'But what do you actually do in this spacious office of yours?'

His jibe focused her attention once more, and she straightened her spine, forced her head up higher. 'I imagine you've already discussed the staff and our responsibilities with Sofia.'

The pen kept tapping.

'I want to hear it from you.'

It was impossible not to feel intimidated by the man. From the edge of her desk he dominated the space before her, looming large and much too close. She looked up at him, feeling her eyes narrow as she tried to work out where he was coming from. No doubt he already had plans in mind for the company. Where did she fit in with those plans?

She needed this job. With a brand-new mortgage to her name, the first chance she'd had to find a real home for her and Jason, now she needed it more than ever. Aristos hadn't been the easiest boss, but the chance to get out of their poky flat and into a real house with a real backyard was worth anything her former boss had been able to dish out. Now that Nick was the boss, what would he dish out?

'All right. I'm Financial Administrator for the Xenophon Group. I've been here for almost two years, though I haven't been doing this job all that time.'

The pen stopped tapping. 'No. That's what Sofia said. You started out on Reception—is that right?'

Before she could answer she noticed the beat of the pen start up again and felt herself frown. If he was trying to get on her nerves he was doing an excellent job.

'But then the previous two accountants left...?' The query was apparent in his eyes. 'They were no good?'

She shook her head. 'I'm sorry, but your uncle wasn't the easiest person to get on with. He was a demanding boss.'

'My uncle started out with nothing and built a fortune in property worth millions. Of course he would expect a lot from his employees.'

'Of course he did. And he got that—and more. But he was difficult as a boss. Impossible at times. If he was in the office he was shouting. In both cases they were good accountants, but Aristos was always shouting at them for one thing or another—I don't think he trusted them to look after his affairs—and they just got sick of it. In the end they walked out, one after the other. The second one only lasted three months. Someone had to fill the gap immediately, and Sofia offered to look after Reception if I would do it. I'd been helping both of them out and it really wasn't such a big deal.'

'And Aristos didn't employ another accountant? Why would he keep a receptionist in such a position of responsibility?'

Alex bristled. 'Maybe because I do the job well.'

He didn't look convinced.

'If it's any consolation, I think Aristos was surprised too. He was intending to advertise, but the employment agency didn't seem too confident they could find the right person for this job—word had got back to them, obviously—and things here were going well. I was already studying for a business diploma at night—so he was relieved not to have to find someone else.'

And pay them accountant's wages. If there was one thing Aristos loved more than bellowing his commands it had been a bargain, and with her he'd got a cheap accountant—even with the extra he'd reluctantly agreed to pay over her former receptionist's salary.

'Funny, but I don't remember the young Alexandra looking forward to spending her life as some beancounter.'

Alex went rigid. She'd relaxed a little, talking about her job, thinking about things present. He'd just transported her slap-bang into the past. A past she'd rather steer clear of now.

'Funny, but I don't think of myself as a "beancounter".' She ploughed on, ignoring the black look he threw her. 'Besides, I don't think I knew what I wanted back then.'

She certainly hadn't known what she'd *need* back then. Had had no idea she'd have a son to support with no chance of finishing school for years. Had never realised how hard it would be to try and manage time with her son when she had a full-time job and night school study. Hadn't known how hard it would be to earn enough money to put a deposit on an ageing two-bedroom bungalow in the suburbs.

He tapped the pen loudly once more, this time on her desk, snapping her out of her thoughts. 'And Aristos didn't shout at you?'

She laughed a little, relieved he was talking about the more recent past once more. 'Sure, he shouted. He shouted at everyone—including Sofia. But as a property investor, he wrote the book. I learned a lot working for him.'

It was true. It might have been unbearable, just as it had proved for the former employees, except she'd needed the money and the experience more. A few years in this job and she'd be finished with her diploma and could get a decent job with better pay. Aristos had given her a chance and she'd grasped it. For all his faults, he'd at least given her this opportunity, and she owed him for that.

But Aristos was gone, and it was his nephew now sitting in front of her. And yet still she hadn't even offered the merest of condolences.

'The news about your uncle must have come as quite a shock. I'm sorry...'

He watched her for a second, but it was as if his eyes were shuttered. Then he slammed the pen down on the desk in the same instant as he heaved himself away. He took a few steps, one hand rubbing his nape.

'It was a shock—but nothing compared to what Sofia is contending with. To have lost her mother to cancer a decade ago, and now to lose her father so suddenly…' He sighed, and for a moment looked so lost in his own thoughts that she sensed there was more to his statement than just compassion for his cousin.

He turned suddenly to face her, his eyes dark and fathomless. 'My mother, Helena, was step-sister to Aristos. She died some six years back herself. Aristos and my father were as close as brothers while they were both alive, even though I didn't know him that well.'

Alex swallowed. She'd never met Nick's parents— but she'd heard enough about his father way back then to scare her socks off. It came as no surprise that he was related, even by marriage, to Aristos.

Even so, they had been Nick's parents. *Jason's grandparents*. And now he would never have the opportunity to meet them. Guilt stabbed deeper inside her.

When would she stop paying for the decision she'd made so long ago? The decision she knew was the right one.

'Your parents…I didn't know…' She shook her head. 'What happened to your father?'

'Why should you know?' he asked sharply, as if she had no right. Then his voice softened. 'About two years ago now he drove off a bridge. Drowned before he could be rescued.'

'That's awful,' said Alex. When they'd been on Crete both Nick's and her own parents had been alive. It had been less than nine years ago and now Nick's parents had gone. How long before hers too were no longer here?

She'd see them at Christmas, when they were planning to travel across the country from Perth to visit. But that was still weeks away. She'd call them tonight. The thought that they wouldn't be there for ever...it was unimaginable.

To be so alone... She sucked in a breath. As she had countless times before, she thanked her lucky stars her sister Tilly had also chosen to make her home in Sydney, to pursue her growing wedding planner career. At least she had some family close by. For all that she was struggling to make ends meet, at least she had someone to turn to, someone to give her moral support when things got too bad. Sofia had no one. And nor, it seemed, did Nick.

'I really am sorry. I had no idea.'

Nick stopped pacing and stood, propping his arms on the back of the visitor's chair. His exhale came out like a sigh. 'In a way it was a release for my father. I think he'd stopped living years before, when Stavros died.' His eyes bore the pain of loss and tragedy, and as they sought and found hers something connected between them.

He remembered. She could tell.

It was the last time they'd spoken. She'd rung, flushed with excitement at her news. After months of hiding the truth she'd finally held her baby—*their baby*—and known that in spite of all the powerful reasons why she shouldn't tell him she simply had to. He had a right to know he was a father. That he had a son.

Only when she'd finally made the connection to Nick's house it had been to find the family in mourning for the eldest son.

How did you say, *I'm sorry your brother is dead and congratulations—today you became a father* in the same sentence? How did you drop a bombshell like that into a grieving family and expect them to embrace a new branch of the family they didn't know existed and wouldn't want to know? Not after what had happened to Stavros.

Realising that no one in his family would ever believe her, let alone welcome her news, Alex had hung up the phone, keeping her secret and knowing she'd never speak to Nick again.

Stavros had been killed, Nick had become the new heir to the family fortune, and it had been obvious there could never be a future with Nick—neither for her nor their newborn child.

Alex rubbed her arms. It was cold in here. She'd have to check the wall thermostat. But not now. Not until Nick had left her office and there was no chance of getting anywhere near him.

His eyes narrowed until they glinted and he straightened behind the chair.

'Something frightened you away. Is that it? Is that why you never returned my calls after that?' His words speared through her consciousness to places she'd rather not go. It was one thing to know she'd done the right thing. It was another thing entirely to have to explain it.

'Nick, I don't think we need to rehash all that. It's in the past. Let it stay there.'

'No. I think the least you can do is offer me an explanation.'

Alex stiffened in her chair. What relationship they'd had had been over for the better part of nine years, and here he was, larger than life, insisting on the whys and wherefores. Talk about inflated male ego! As if it mattered now.

'Let it go—'

'Was it another man?' He threw a glance to her left hand. 'You're not married, but was there someone back then?'

'Look, it's not important—'

'So it *was* another man. Why else would you just stop communicating? I tried to call you. I wrote to you.'

'We moved—'

'*I* didn't. You knew where to find me.' Accusation was layered thickly in his eyes. 'So why else would you never return my calls? Why never answer my letters unless you were too busy in someone else's bed?'

Enough! Incensed, Alex pushed herself up from her chair. She'd had enough of looking up to him. And she was sick of putting up with his slurs.

'Drop it, Nick.'

'I demand to know what happened!'

Alex glared at him, at that moment totally wondering how she'd ever held the notion that she'd loved this guy. 'I grew up.' *The hard way.* 'End of story.'

'It's no wonder you've never married, if that's the way you treat men. If you want my advice—'

Alex's hands curled into tight fists.

'As a matter of fact,' she cut in, 'I don't want your advice. I don't need your advice. And, given that you don't appear to be married either, are you completely sure you're in any position to give advice?'

In that moment Nick's face might have been cast from concrete. It seemed all harsh angles and rigid planes, and she could tell he was battling to keep the fury he was obviously feeling under control.

Well, bully for him. She was furious too. How dared the brute think he could waltz back into her life and start criticising?

A muscle in his cheek twitched. 'You've changed, Alexandra. You are still as beautiful as you were then, maybe even more so, but you've changed on the inside.'

I've had to! Her mind told her to remain strong and

resolute. It shouldn't matter what he said about her looks. And it wouldn't. *She wouldn't let it.*

She sucked in one unsteady breath, battled to get her speech back to something resembling normality. 'Please leave. I have work to do.'

When he remained there motionless it was obvious that he had no intention of complying with her request. If she wanted him out of her office she was going to have to make him leave herself.

She stepped around the desk. 'I'll see you to the door.'

There was at least four feet between them and she'd mentally assessed the risk. There was no chance of them coming close to each other. In a moment she'd be safely behind the open door, ushering him out, and some sort of peace could again reign in her office.

Halfway there his hand seized her arm, halting her in her tracks. His grip burned, his hand looking so large on her forearm that her heart tripped. She'd known that touch before, known the strength of it, and yet the tenderness that could accompany it. Only there was none of that tenderness now. Now she sensed anger, and her heart raced fast and loud as adrenalin kicked in once again.

'Alexandra,' he said, half demanding, yet half imploring. She closed her eyes briefly and willed herself not to be affected by the mere sound of her name.

'Let me go.' Her voice sounded amazingly calm and level and she took strength from that.

But he didn't let go. His grip changed. Instead of

just holding her, it was tugging her, forcing her closer
to him. They were close enough now that she could
catch the tang of his subtle cologne, the faint remnants of his coffee, all infused with the scent of
man—angry man.

'Alexandra?'

Her elbow was still locked, her arm held firm, as
she looked up into his eyes. Breath caught in her
throat as anger was replaced by something else.
Something darker and far more dangerous.

In that instant he relaxed his hold, and with the
pressure off she immediately lost balance, swaying on
her heels, only to be pulled unceremoniously back
into him in the next moment.

Impacting against his chest was like colliding with
solid rock—only warm and smooth and, oh, so familiar. She sucked in a deep breath, her senses reeling
from so much male so close. Something in the back
of her mind registered that Nick hadn't changed that
much. Somehow this was just the way she remembered he'd felt back then. Maybe just a little broader
and more developed, but just the way she'd imagined,
late at night when she couldn't sleep, thinking how
he'd feel now.

Only this was all wrong!

'Let me go!' she urged, trying to push him away.
But his arms snaked around her, holding her tight.

She pulled her head back to look up at him. 'What
the hell do you think you're doing? This is harassment. You can't try these caveman tactics here.'

'Harassment?' His tone mocked and his eyes held a teasing glint.

An unkind, teasing glint she registered. Life had apparently left Nick bitter.

Then she realised he was moving, swaying ever so gently, the fingers of his hands stroking her back while his arms still kept their vice-like grip. The motion was disarming, gently soothing and strangely sensual.

'Hardly harassment,' he went on. 'Don't you remember how it was between us? We're simply sharing an embrace, and perhaps a kiss for old times' sake.'

Alarm bells went off in her head. *No way.* No way would she kiss him. He couldn't be serious.

Firmly she pressed her hands against Nick's chest and pushed for all she was worth. 'I have no intention of sharing *anything* with you.'

He must have seen something in her face because he looked down at her strangely, stopped swaying and abruptly let her go. Alex wheeled away before he had a chance to change his mind, her breath coming thick and fast. She grabbed hold of the door handle and screwed it round, yanking open the door for him.

He stood for a moment, taking a couple of deep breaths. He strode to the door, came so close to her she was afraid he might just kiss her anyway. 'There was once a time you would beg me to kiss you, again and again.'

She pushed back her shoulders, tried as best as she

could to look him in the eye—even though he had a head start of six inches on her.

'Times have changed.'

He reached out a hand and she flinched, but his fingers moved to the side of her face to tuck behind her ear a strand that had come loose from her twisted up hair. She swallowed, otherwise motionless, as they traced a path down her cheek before he gently but firmly pinched her chin between his thumb and forefinger.

'Not for the better, it seems.'

He flicked off his fingers and she fumbled for something to say.

'I...I'll get some financial statements ready for you. I guess you'll want to get things organised quickly, to allow you to get back to Greece as soon as you can.'

She could swear he almost smiled then. A smile that didn't touch anywhere near his eyes.

'Who said anything about going home to Greece? I may just decide to stay the full six months Aristos's will requires.'

Then he was finally gone. Alex shut the door and let herself collapse against it. It was barely eleven in the morning and she felt as if she'd just run a marathon.

How in the world would she survive six months?

CHAPTER FOUR

ALEX stood on the sidelines, clutching her thirty-eight-millimetre camera and waiting while the coach said a few final words to the team, grateful that Sofia had chosen this particular afternoon to show Nick around some of their properties, allowing her to slip off half an hour early unnoticed.

After an emotionally draining day Alex was more anxious than ever to be with her son. This was *their* night—hers and Jason's—with no study or classes to intrude. Just for now she'd rather not have to explain that to Nick.

She took a couple of deep breaths and rolled her shoulders, easing away some of the strain of the day, before putting the cap back on the camera lens. She'd taken enough shots today to fill another page in the album she was keeping—the albums and video recordings she was using to record every event and growth phase in Jason's life.

The albums and videos she was one day intending to show his father.

Only his father was here. *Now*.

How the hell was she supposed to deal with that? Somehow she had to work out a way of coping with Nick's presence in the office. It was only day one, but from the tension evident between them today it was difficult to believe they could ever work together comfortably as colleagues. It certainly wasn't going to happen with this huge secret hanging over them.

If he was ever going to see these pictures and videos, eventually—inevitably—she'd have to tell him the truth. Only things were so complicated. Now she couldn't just tell him about their son. Now she'd also have to explain why she had never told him at the start. Never told him she was pregnant with his child. Never told him he was a father.

And there was no easy way to do it.

Yet the longer Nick stayed, the more inevitable it would become that he would find out she had a son. Once he knew she had a son…how long would it take before he worked out the rest and know she had kept the truth from him?

Her heart kicked up a beat. Just maybe there was a chance Nick wouldn't see the resemblance. Close relatives didn't always notice such things, did they? After all, people were always telling her that in spite of Jason's dark hair and eyes he was still unmistakably hers, even though she couldn't see it herself. Maybe Nick would be the same?

She looked closer at the huddle of players. Jason had his head cocked to one side, listening intently to the coach's words, concentrating hard, his eyes dark and intense, and as she looked at him a chill whipped up her spine.

Her son stood there focused and determined—

every part a miniature version of Nick. Alex took a deep breath and tried to steady her heartbeat back into a normal rhythm.

She'd been kidding herself. There was no way Nick could deny the resemblance. She sighed. That left only one course of action. It wasn't going to be easy, but she'd have to do it—and the sooner the better.

The team huddle broke up and Jason turned and waved, smiling as he ran towards her until he collided at force into her chest, swinging her with his momentum. She breathed in the happy, warm smell of him, mingled with grass and earth, and caught his laughter as he clutched on tightly around her neck and they spun each other round.

'Pizza!' he squealed.

She laughed and stood up, catching his hand in hers as she turned to the car. 'I hope you spent some time out there thinking about soccer, and not just what you wanted for dinner.'

'Yeah,' he said, tugging her along. 'A bit.'

Four pieces of pizza later, Jason started to slow down between bites. After a brief hesitation he reached for his cola and took a long drink. 'Can you fish, Mum?'

Alex blinked and put her piece down. It was noisy in the pizza bar and she wasn't sure she'd heard correctly. 'You mean with a rod and reel?'

Jason nodded and studied the remaining pieces before reaching for the one with the most olives, despite it being the furthest away.

'I've been known to catch the odd fish, sure.'

Jason focused on his next mouthful before continuing. 'I thought so. I told them you could do anything, but they still said I couldn't come.'

'You told who? And couldn't come where?' she asked, secretly pleased that Jason still had such faith in her.

'Matt and Jack. They're going fishing one weekend with their dads. They said I could have come but you were a girl and you wouldn't know how to fish.'

'That's a shame,' she said, feeling more than slightly put out. 'Did you want to go?'

'Sort of. The camping out sounded the best bit, though.'

'Ah,' she said, getting some idea of the real reason why they might be uncomfortable with a woman along. 'I know why they didn't want us to go.'

'Why?'

She smiled. 'Well, how would they feel when we caught all the fish?'

'I knew it.' Jason leaned back in his chair and surveyed with only half interest the few remnants left in the pizza box. 'I told them it wouldn't make any difference even if I had a dad, because we'd still catch the most too.' Then he burped loudly, clapped his hand over his mouth and collapsed into a fit of giggles.

Alex laughed too, but inside felt his words as a boot to her heart. Hot tears stung her eyes.

It's the shock, she tried to tell herself as she

brushed away the evidence with the back of her hand, pretending they were laughter induced. Naturally she would be feeling more sensitive than usual after Aristos's sudden death and the arrival of Nick on the scene. Why else would she be crying into her pizza at dinnertime?

But, despite what she wanted to believe, part of her knew there was more to her tears than that. Once again she was reminded that no matter how she tried to be both mother and father to Jason, to provide him with the balance his young life required, there would be times when she just couldn't be both.

Jet lag, Nick decided. It had to be jet lag.

Why else would his legs be so unresponsive and his body so stressed and lethargic? Three kilometres into his run along the foreshore, it was obvious he wasn't going to make his usual ten. The rhythm wasn't there, his breathing was forced, and the power just wasn't happening.

And he needed to run. Needed to clear the fog that was clouding his brain, the fog that sprang from changing time zones and hemispheres—and from a girl he should have forgotten long ago.

Who was he trying to kid? She was hardly a girl any more. One touch had confirmed that. His breath caught in his throat, he coughed and shot his rhythm to hell again. In rebellion, he cursed, kicking out one foot at the sand, spraying the heavy salt-encrusted grains far and wide, scattering seagulls up into the ever lightening sky.

Breath rasped and scratched his throat. He needed sleep. Long, uninterrupted sleep. Instead last night he'd been plagued with visions of a leggy teenager, sitting cross-legged and smiling up at him from the midst of a field of yellow wild flowers, her long blonde hair almost liquid in the gentle spring breeze.

She'd been nervous. But she'd come to meet him willingly, knowing that this was the day—their last together—and her shyness had faded under his touch and they'd taken each other to a place they'd always share.

Or so he'd thought.

Maybe he'd got it wrong back then. From the way Alexandra acted now, it was clear she wasn't interested in sharing the time of day with him. He smiled to himself.

The way she'd reacted when he'd suggested staying in Australia! She obviously couldn't wait for him to get out of her life. He didn't even know why he'd said that; he had no intention of staying here. Although it was more than obvious that Sofia was keen he should hang around a while.

Maybe he should.

So far Dimitri was insisting that all was well with the business in Athens, and it was clear that Sofia needed his support here. Maybe that wouldn't be as onerous as he'd first expected. Somewhere along the line Sofia had transformed herself from a pestering child into a dark-haired beauty. Perhaps it wouldn't hurt him to stick around a while—at least until she'd had time to come to terms with her loss.

A thin smile found its way to his lips as another reason to stay crystallised. For there was something infinitely satisfying about making Alexandra think she was not going to be rid of him too easily.

But then, that was foolish thinking. He wasn't here to settle scores. He was here to make sure the business functioned well and prospered long into the future. He should be thinking instead whether there was even a place for her in the operation.

If he was going to leave the business in sound hands it was clear there'd have to be someone pretty damned capable in the financial area. Would a receptionist-cum-bookkeeper make the grade? He doubted it. It might be better to get someone better qualified in and just let her go. Although the employment agencies had had no success so far.

Maybe it would be better getting Dimitri to come out from Greece. He would know what the job required, so they could employ the right person.

Gulls wheeled overhead and a lonely swimmer hauled himself from the water nearby, shaking jewelled droplets from his body as he surged out of the shallows.

A swim. Maybe that was what Nick needed to clear his head of this infernal jet lag. Lord knows, the run didn't seem to be helping. He turned back the way he had come and headed along the beach.

*   *   *

'He's cute, don't you think?'

Alex looked up from her computer screen, in the middle of typing her letter. 'Who's cute?' she asked innocently, keeping her face deliberately schooled as she minimised her computer screen. But Sofia was too busy closing the door to notice anything. She grabbed one of the visitor's chairs by the arm and pulled it up close to the desk, hunkering down conspiratorially, her elbows on the desk, cupping her chin. She was grinning from ear to ear.

'Nick, silly. Who else around here could I mean?'

Alex smiled indulgently. While 'cute' wasn't exactly the word that sprang to mind whenever she thought about Nick, it was obvious who Sofia was referring to. Apart from the two of them, the office only employed a part-time woman for the phones, for whenever Sofia had had enough of playing receptionist, and an ageing property manager who looked after maintenance issues.

Still, she feigned surprise. 'Oh, him. Sure, he's not bad.'

It was easy to play along. Sofia was the happiest she'd seen her since her father had died. If having Nick here did that for her, then at least something good would come from his visit. With no one else to turn to, Sofia deserved it.

'I think he likes me.'

Alex's breath snagged in her throat. *Oh, please, I don't want to hear this!*

She somehow forced a bare smile to her face. 'Of course he likes you. You're his cousin. You're a nice girl. Why wouldn't he like you?'

She shook her head. 'No, you don't get what I mean. I mean he *likes* me. You know—like, seriously likes me.'

'That's…nice.' Alex wondered what else she was expected to say. She looked at the girl sitting opposite, her dark eyes shining with hope in her impeccably made-up face, her insanely long acrylic fingernails painted the exact shade of her crimson lips.

Sofia had never had the greatest history with boyfriends, and little wonder, given her domineering father and his ability to drive away potential suitors with a single bellow. If only his interest had been motivated by his daughter's welfare. Instead, Alex suspected, he'd always had the future of the Xenophon Group foremost in his mind. Whoever married his daughter and sole heir would end up with the fruits of Aristos's labour. How could any mere male qualify for such bountiful reward?

And then along came Nick, apparently with Daddy's blessing, and for the first time in her life Sofia thought she was onto a winner.

Sofia and Nick. Why did that seem such an unlikely pairing? And why should she even care? It wasn't as if she had any claim on the man, after all.

'I was wondering,' Sofia said, 'if you could help me—while he's out for a little while, talking to some of the tenants?' She tilted her head to one side, making her large gold double-hoop earrings jangle. 'See-ing you know Nick much better than me, what with being old friends and all.'

Alex shook her head. 'You've got the wrong idea. That was a long time ago.'

'But I haven't seen him since I was six, and he hardly took any notice of me. Even though way back then I thought he was gorgeous. I just thought you might have some idea of what he likes, you know. You must have talked about something when you were in Crete together. What did you guys get up to anyway?'

The breath left Alex's lungs so fast it made her cough. What on earth would Sofia think if she told her the truth? *I gave him my virginity and he took me to heaven.* No, definitely more information than Sofia needed to know. And much more information than Alex needed to be reminded of. Besides, they had done other things on Crete—it was just hard to focus on them now. Now that Nick was here. She licked her lips, buying time.

'You know—the usual things one does over there. We visited ruins and museums. Remember, Nick was studying an archaeology unit back then. No doubt he's still interested in the subject. Why don't you ask him about it?'

Sofia screwed up her nose. 'I guess. But that's not really what I had in mind.' She fidgeted with her ban-gles, then checked her nails. 'I don't know—does he have a favourite colour or something?'

Alex smiled to herself, instantly transported back to Crete.

Nick was holding her face in his hands, his lips close to hers, and the breeze was floating tendrils of her unbound hair around them both.

'The colour of the ocean, deep and clear. The colour of the sky, bright and endless. The colour of your eyes…'

She shook her head before she could think too much about the kiss that had followed.

'Blue.'

'Cool!' Sofia flicked her glance to her watch. 'I have to go shopping. He's taking me out to dinner tonight, and I just feel I need to get into something a little less—black.' She paused and pressed her lips together tightly, her eyes filmed with tears. 'It's just so hard being reminded all the time.'

'It's bound to be. A shopping trip is probably just what you need—but can I get you anything now?'

Sofia sniffed, and dabbed at her eyes with a tissue. 'No. I'll be fine. I have to get going. Nick and I have a lot of things to organise with the company and everything. You know how it is.' She rose and headed for the door, but halfway through stopped and turned around. 'He asked if you were coming, but I told him you probably wouldn't be able to get a babysitter at such short notice. He didn't seem to know you had a kid. You haven't told him?'

He knows!

Ice formed in her veins, yet somehow she managed to force her jaw to work.

'Ah. No, not yet. We haven't had much chance so far to catch up, that's all.'

Another sniff and a shrug later Sofia was gone. Alex sat stunned, her breathing shallow and fast, her mind racing.

He knows.

But how much did he know? How much had Sofia told him? She'd never shown much interest in children in general or in Jason in particular. What could she have given away? Maybe there was still time.

In a flash she maximised her computer screen and finished typing the letter before printing it off. She read it through once more and nodded. Perfect. All it needed was her signature.

She was doing the right thing; she was sure of it.

In a moment it was signed and sealed and ready to be dropped off on Nick's desk before he was back from seeing the tenants.

She took a deep breath and, suddenly parched, reached for her glass of water. It was empty. She stopped by the small office kitchenette to fill it, popping the envelope on the adjacent benchtop while she poured the cool spring water. She was standing at the dispenser, with her back to the door, when she felt it.

Something wasn't right.

Hairs prickled on the back of her neck and her heart belted out an erratic beat that reverberated in her head, spelling out exactly how she felt. *Scared.*

Quickly she turned, feeling his presence before there was so much as a sound.

Water sloshed over the glass's rim, but she hardly noticed or cared. 'Nick! You startled me.'

He was leaning against the doorway, hands in pockets. Strange how even in such a casual stance Nick could look all man. Relaxed, comfortable—*predatory*.

Slowly he peeled himself away from the doorway and moved closer.

There was no telling what he was thinking. His dark eyes were unfathomable. He stopped a couple of feet in front of her, filling all the remaining space in the tiny kitchenette. She swallowed. Until Nick moved she was stuck here, with a brimming glass of water the only thing between them. As defences went, it wasn't much, but somehow just holding it there made her feel better. If only she could hold her hand steady.

'Sofia took me for a tour of the properties yesterday.'

'Yes, I heard.'

'It's a large portfolio. I was impressed by the quality of the holdings.'

'That's good.'

Alex winced at her lame responses, but how was she supposed to concentrate with him in the room? It was all she could do to keep her hand from shaking and spilling some more water.

'I imagine it takes quite a bit of accounting skill to keep up with it all.'

'Not really,' she said, studying the glass and using all her powers of concentration to will it to stay level. 'Once the systems are in place—' *What am I thinking?* If he wanted to imply that she couldn't do the job, it would be in her interests to agree with him. She jerked her eyes up to meet his.

'Actually, you're right. It's very complic—'

Nick jumped back before the wave of spring water could collect him fair in the chest, and Alex realised she hadn't just kicked up her chin when she'd changed her response.

Even with his quick evasive action the water landed at his feet, beading droplets over the sculpted black leather of his Italian shoes. In a flash he relieved her of the glass, and its remaining contents, and deposited it on the benchtop alongside the letter—*his letter* while she stood there dumbfounded.

'You're jumpy, Alexandra.'

She looked up at him, preparing to apologise, but he took her shoulders in his large hands. Instantly every cell in her body seemed to contract and freeze.

'Do I make you so nervous?'

She sucked in a necessary breath—only to find the oxygen she so desperately required infused with the scent of this man. Heat replaced the coldness she'd been feeling, warming sensations and desires she'd thought long buried. Under her discount designer jacket and tailored shirt her breasts felt swollen and firm, aware of even the slightest brush of fabric over the points of her bra. And now that feeling coiled downwards, stirring feelings long since forgotten.

She sighed. There seemed little point in denying it. 'Yes, I guess you do.'

He laughed, softly and openly, his breath curling warm against her face as his thumbs gently traced the line of her collarbone, almost hypnotising her. The flesh tingled under his touch. Alex felt her eyelids flutter. Oh, God! He hadn't forgotten how to make her feel good, just as her body hadn't forgotten how to respond to his.

'But why, Alexandra, should I make you nervous? I am just a man. A man who, after all, you know— intimately.'

Something about the way he spoke made her look at him—really look at him. Why was he doing this to her? She willed her body not to be carried away by his touch, but that same body seemed intent on ignoring her. After all, this was just what she'd dreamed of, night after lonely night—being with Nick, enjoying his touch. Now her dreams had become reality, at least in part, and it was so hard to deny herself that for which she'd yearned so long.

Only she had to. Her lips felt desperate for moisture as she finally spoke.

'That was a long time ago. It's ancient history now.'

'Maybe. But sometimes the past can pave the way for the future. We were once good together. Is there any reason why we shouldn't be again—at least until I leave?'

'What?'

She dropped a shoulder and twisted out of his reach before he could react.

For just one moment his words had brought her an unexpected pleasure. For just one moment it had seemed he might still harbour some feelings for her.

In the next moment he'd shattered the illusion. 'Just what are you suggesting?'

He shrugged and leaned himself back against the cupboards, crossing his ankles, his hands resting on the bench behind. The relaxed position belied the expression on his face. His jaw was set and his eyes looked more calculating than ever.

'Simply that we fit together well—you know that. Why shouldn't we seek pleasure in each other? There's little enough to be found elsewhere in this world.'

'You expect me to sleep with you while you're here?'

He looked over at her, his lips tilted at one corner, his dark eyes resolute as he pushed himself away from the bench and took two paces towards her.

Instinctively her feet edged back.

'No, Alexandra. You have the wrong idea entirely. I don't expect you to sleep with me. I want you awake, very much awake. I don't expect we should get very much sleep at all.'

Alex could only swallow as he moved a step closer,

and then another, forcing her back against the small under-counter refrigerator. Only then did he stop—right in front of her.

'After all,' he continued, 'it's not as if you are a virgin, as I can attest. You're not married, and you've obviously had other partners. Sofia told me of your child. You expect me to believe that was the result of immaculate conception?'

Hot, angry tears pricked her eyes. Even if he didn't know that the child he referred to was his, there was no excuse for speaking to her that way. 'And that makes it okay, then, does it? I should be only too willing to fall into your bed?'

His eyes held hers as he curled one hand around one hip and then the other. Alex flinched, surprised by the move, and grabbed his forearms, trying to push them away. But his arms were like steel and couldn't be budged.

'I know the way I feel when I touch you. I know the way you respond to that touch. Can you deny that you would like me to touch you even more?'

He pulled her closer, making a mockery of her resistance.

'Can you deny that you want me in your bed?'

Alex felt his arms slide up behind her, pulling them even closer together.

He was right, in so many ways. His touch now was so much like it had been years before—firm, warm, *hot*. Back then one touch hadn't been enough. One touch had never been enough. Not when it had sparked desire and want and need. She couldn't deny that she would like him in her bed—hadn't she dreamed of just that over the last years?—but their lovemaking had never been callous then, and she wouldn't let it be reduced to that now.

Not when there was so much at stake.

Her face close to his, she delivered her answer in the steadiest voice she could muster. 'You're wrong. I don't want you in my bed.'

'Liar,' he said, smiling. 'Your body gives me a different answer.'

Before he'd finished talking he'd slipped one hand below her jacket, sliding it across the silk of her shirt and up to capture her breast. Her breath hissed in as his thumb almost casually stroked the peak of one hardened nipple. With his other hand he pulled her even closer to him, pressing her against his obvious hardness.

'Now tell me you don't want me.'

Alex's tongue met parched, dry lips as she battled to find strength she didn't feel. 'I don't want you— not like this.'

Her voice trembled, and without slackening his hold he stared down at her, disbelieving.

'Never like this,' she added, stronger this time.

A second later his hands slid out from under her jacket and he shrugged.

He'd let her go. But there was no time to congratulate herself—not before Nick was on the attack once more.

'So you might feel like this now. But have you realised just how hard it is going to be for you to keep denying this attraction between us as we work together, day after day?'

He smiled, looking entirely like a man sure he had just delivered his trump card. Alex gulped in air, trying to replace the oxygen he had scorched with just his touch.

'I don't see why that should be a problem,' she said in barely a whisper as she reached around him to retrieve the envelope. She held it up to him. 'Maybe you should read this.'

He looked at the blank envelope suspiciously. 'What's this?'

For the first time since his arrival Alex felt she had Nick at a disadvantage. It was a pleasant change, and one that brought a bittersweet smile to her face.

'My resignation,' she said. 'I'm leaving, Nick.'

CHAPTER FIVE

HE HELD the envelope, not opening it, all the while just glaring at her. Alex waited, the initial rush of adrenalin at delivering what should have been the killer punch evaporating as time strung out between them. When he finally spoke his words were barely more than an order.

'You can't.'

'Open it,' she urged. 'Read it.'

'You can't resign.'

'You don't want me here. You've made it plain you don't think I'm qualified to do the job. Well, you're right. You'd be much better off finding someone else.'

His head tilted to one side, his eyes sceptical. 'You don't believe that.'

Her shoulders lifted in a shrug, but that didn't mean she was ready to give in to him.

'What does it matter what I believe? I'm making it easy for you. I'm resigning. Now you're free to get in someone who you're sure can do the job.'

His eyes narrowed, calculating, *dangerous*, and then, without breaking eye contact, he ripped the envelope in two.

'What are you doing?' she cried in disbelief as he

tore it through again and scattered the pieces with a flick of his wrist in the general direction of the bin.

'Simple. I'm not accepting your resignation. You're staying.'

'I'm going. I'll print another copy, and another, if that's what it takes.'

'Don't bother. I'll do the same with them.'

'You can't make me stay.'

'I don't need to. You've done that yourself.'

'What do you mean?'

'Simple. You have a contract, Alexandra. A contract for two years, with more than eighteen months to run. And I'm holding you to it.'

Alex sucked in a sharp breath.

'I have no contract with you.'

'Your contract is with the Xenophon Group, and right now that means me.'

'But you don't want me here. Why are you doing this?'

'Because you know the company, Alexandra. Even when we get a qualified accountant to take over you will no doubt be useful for secretarial and...' his eyes took on a vicious gleam '...any other duties I may require.'

Alex felt as if the breath had been sucked from her, her pulse beating a storm through her veins as the meaning behind his words struck home.

'You can't be serious,' she whispered in a voice that sounded so flat and empty it mirrored her soul.

'Alexandra,' he said simply, as one might speak to

a child who couldn't comprehend something basic, 'you should know I'm *always* serious.'

Watching the lines of his face harden and set, she knew better than to doubt him. His intent was clear in the flare of his nostrils and the arrogant tilt of his jaw.

But he needn't think he had a monopoly on being serious! She gulped in air, fortifying herself for the battle she knew she had on her hands.

'Don't assume that just because I have to stay here I'll be doing anything other than my work. Because I won't.'

He smiled, then leaned back against the bench and twisted the wristband of his watch with his free hand, as if he was bored. That he looked partly amused only served to fuel her anger. She'd do anything to wipe that smile off his face.

'Really?' he said finally. 'And how can you be so sure of yourself?'

'Because, if you haven't already realised,' she replied, lifting her own chin a notch, 'I'm not the naïve seventeen-year-old you met on Crete.'

His smile deepened, his eyes raking over her.

He didn't have to do that. Look at her as if he was assessing just how much the intervening years had changed her, mentally comparing his memories of her then with the reality of her now.

'Just looking at you, I never thought for one moment that you were. But, in any event, I look forward to the challenge.' His eyes glittered, as if he'd won a major battle rather than just readied himself for the skirmish to come.

No doubt he thought it was only a matter of time before she fell into his bed. His arrogance alone was enough to ensure she wouldn't give in to his expectations.

'There's no challenge, Nick. It's a statement of fact. I'm not sleeping with you.'

Without waiting for his response, she willed herself to push past him and exit—only to almost crash into Sofia, laden with shopping bags, returning from her shopping expedition.

'Wait till you see what I've bought,' Sofia said, her smile wide and her cheeks flushed.

Normally Alex wouldn't have had the time or the inclination to be interested, but today was different. Today she could do with the diversion—and a reason for Nick not to follow her.

She smiled with a warmth she didn't feel as she ushered the girl into her office. 'Show me,' she invited, closing the door firmly after them.

'You have to tell him.' Tilly positioned the three sets of knives and forks around the small dining room table as she spoke, and only then looked up at her sister, as if impatient for a response. 'You *will* tell him?'

Alex tried to ignore her sister's glare and busied herself with the plates and salad. She'd made it through a whole week of putting up with Nick's constant presence in the office. A whole week of Nick's needling barbs. A whole week of Nick's dark eyes following her every movement.

One whole week! She wanted to congratulate herself. If she could make it through one week then maybe she could make it through two, or four, or however many weeks it took till he finally went home to Greece.

Couldn't Tilly see that? She was beginning to regret telling her sister anything. Only she'd been bursting to confide in someone. It was simply too much information to keep to herself. She opened the fridge, extracted the salad dressing from the door, and popped it down on the table.

'Alex!' repeated Tilly, sounding more agitated by the minute. 'You are going to tell him. He has a right to know. They *both* have a right to know.'

'Okay, I hear you.' She stole a glance out of the window. 'Is Jason still outside? He needs to wash up.'

'So you'll tell him, then? And Jason?'

Alex sighed and licked a trace of avocado from her fingers. 'You know, Tilly, Nick's going back to Greece. It could be in two months; it could be in two weeks. Is it really fair to tell either of them when Nick could just turn around and walk out of Jason's life?'

'You don't know that. He could decide to stay— and who knows? Maybe he'll even take you both back to Greece with him. I remember he was crazy about you when we were in Crete. You seemed to have the hots for him pretty bad too.'

Alex laughed—a low, brittle laugh. *Take them both back to Greece?* It didn't sound like the action of a man who had offered her casual sex for the duration of his visit. It didn't sound as if she figured in any long-term plans, with or without a child. 'I don't think so. Nick's changed. He seems—bitter—somehow.' She tried to remember the words he'd used—something about there being little pleasure in the world.

Nick had a hard edge that hadn't been there all those years ago. A hard edge no doubt caused by watching his family disappear around him—first his brother, then his mother and father. Aristos's death must have brought it all back in sharp relief.

And was her own hasty departure from their relationship also partly to blame? Nick had needed her and she'd abandoned him, not wanting to cause the family more pain than it already had to deal with. Was he trying to punish her now? To get back at her for that?

It wouldn't be fair if he was. She'd needed him more than ever back then. By denying that need she'd saved them more grief—only how was he to understand that?

'Anyway,' Tilly continued, 'whatever Nick chooses to do after he finds out he has a son—that's irrelevant as far as your decision is concerned. Despite whatever you think his reaction will be, he still has a right to know—and I think you know it.'

'But I have Jason to think of too. He's my first priority now.'

'So think of him! How will he feel if he finds out that his father spent time in Sydney, in close proximity to him, and yet you never told him he was here, let alone introduced him? Don't you think he'll feel just a tiny bit cheated?'

Alex opened her mouth, preparing to defend herself, but it was no good. She snapped it shut. Her sister was right. And when she thought about it that was exactly why she'd told her sister in the first place. Because she knew that Tilly would be impartial. That Tilly, in her naturally analytical way, would assess all the information and come up with what was the most fair, the most moral result. Even if it didn't seem like much of a solution for Alex.

But her sister was spot on. Alex would have to introduce Jason to his father and Nick to his son. Only how the heck was she supposed to do it? Especially with Nick appearing to bear such a grudge against her.

Not that Tilly would be much help there. She'd no doubt say that any interest or uninterest shown in her by Nick was irrelevant too. That Nick and Jason still had to know of each other's existence regardless. And she'd still be right.

Alex sighed. In a way Nick's resentment towards her should make it easier to break the news. He already thought little enough of her. What did she have to lose?

'Yeah, you're right. I'll have to tell them both.'

Tilly stopped, her glass of wine poised halfway to her lips.

'You'll tell them, then—when?'

Alex drew in a deep breath. 'I don't know. I can't just come out with it.'

'Can I make a suggestion, then? It's Jason's birthday in two weeks. Maybe it would be nice if Nick could be here for his party. Then you could all be together, just like a real family.'

Just like a real family! That was a joke. The three of them had never been any sort of family, let alone a real one. Alex nibbled at her lip.

'I don't know. What if Jason doesn't like him? What if Nick hates kids?'

Tilly reached out an arm and squeezed her sister's shoulder. 'So introduce them first. Go for a picnic or something. Anything. Of course you can't make them like each other, but Nick must have some redeeming features, surely?' She gazed at her sister pointedly. 'You certainly used to think so.'

Alex thought back to Crete and to the young man she'd fallen in love with—with his dark hair and dark eyes and a smile that had promised for ever. He'd been generous, kind and patient, and in no way flaunting his obvious wealth. She'd been in awe of his sheer magnetism, acutely aware even then of how her body responded to his, whether at a touch or a mere glance.

And Nick now? He seemed a world away from that young man—harder, more cynical—and yet still able to set her body alight with one look. Did pure sexual magnetism qualify as a redeeming feature?

No. It just made him all the more dangerous. But for Jason's sake she really hoped Nick still retained some of that generosity of spirit he'd displayed all those years ago. They were all going to need it.

The back door slammed and the tornado that was her son bowled into the house. 'What's for dinner, Mum? I'm starving.'

Alex smiled and stepped into the kitchen, relieved at the change of subject. 'Lasagne,' she said, opening the oven door, 'and it's ready, so go wash up.' She watched his rapidly departing back and shook her head.

How the hell was she going to tell him?

Tilly followed her into the kitchen, picked up the pile of plates and hesitated, as if sensing her sister's mood.

'You can do this,' she said.

Alex gently smoothed out the folds in the old papers with the flat of her hand, wishing she could iron out the creases in her own life just as easily. Her mouth twitched into a smile. *Some hope.* If anything, her life was about to get a whole lot rougher.

She looked down at the collection of letters and the pile of envelopes lying alongside the mussed ribbon and the old chocolate box she'd found after Tilly had gone home—when she was supposed to be putting away the laundry.

Letters from Nick. *Love letters.*

She looked at the stack of towels and sheets, still sunshine-fresh, sitting neglected on the floor nearby. She'd put them away in a moment—just as soon as she'd read one or two. She'd shoved the box in the back of the cupboard when she'd moved in, refusing to think about its contents. Now it seemed impossible to ignore.

Casting an eye through the nearby French doors, and satisfying herself that Jason, freshly bathed, was still happily attending to his weekend homework, Alex started to read.

The ink was faded in parts, and the words were sometimes difficult to make out in the folds, but the meaning and intent of the letters were crystal-clear, and as she began to read the years faded away.

She smiled when she looked over his earliest letters, written soon after their shared holiday. They were full of optimistic talk about how the archaeological dig he'd been working on in Crete had finished, what he was doing at university, how he missed her and when next they would have the chance to be together again.

In the months that followed the letters contained more family talk. He was increasingly worried about his brother, and the rift between him and his father over his unhappy marriage, and his anger at the woman who had forced him into it. He still missed Alex madly, he said, and worried that her letters seemed more distant, less personal.

Alex sighed as a single tear squeezed its entry into the world. He'd been right. She'd known about the baby coming by then, and known she couldn't tell him. Towards the end of the pregnancy she'd found it hard to write at all. It had been too hard to write small talk when she was keeping the biggest secret she'd ever had from the one who had a right to know but wouldn't want to.

Alex sighed again and turned up one untidily scrawled letter. She looked at the date. He'd sent it after Stavros's funeral. He must have been crying when he wrote it, and his tears had smudged the ink where they fell. It was such a pained letter. He was mourning for his brother, and at the same time mourning for what they'd lost. He seemed to sense that their relationship was over, and was reaching out in one last bid for Alex to give him something she'd desperately wanted to but now never could.

The one time he'd really needed her, she hadn't been able to help. The only fair thing she could do was set him free. So the family couldn't be tainted by another scandalous pregnancy.

There were more letters, but increasingly less frequent after that. Alex skimmed through their content, noted the bitterness that infused his final words.

He'd finished with her. Who could blame him? She'd betrayed his trust. And all because of a secret—a secret bigger than both of them.

Now that secret was almost eight years old—her one link with happier times and a season of love.

Eight years old. And on every one of those birthdays she'd looked at Jason and wondered if she'd done the right thing, wondered if she should have told Nick, whether she should tell him now.

But she only had to look at the words of his final letters. He didn't want to hear from her. He didn't want anything more to do with her.

And his circumstances hadn't changed. After what his family had been through they would never believe her child was Nick's.

She came back to the roughly scrawled letter and its pained contents, and as she read the words over again her heart squeezed so tight that two plump tears rolled down her face, blurring her vision so she barely noticed it when they landed on the page, her tears mingling with his in the smudged ink.

'Mum—what's wrong?' Jason asked. 'What are all those?'

Alex wiped her eyes with the back of her hand and sniffed. 'Oh, just some old letters from a one-time friend of mine,' she said as she hurriedly scrabbled the papers and envelopes together, without bothering to match letters with envelopes.

'So why are you crying?'

'Because I'm happy thinking about those times, silly.' She rose to her feet, congratulating herself on how light she'd managed to sound, and turned towards her bedroom, the bundle of letters, envelopes and the chocolate box trailing its blue satin ribbon in her arms.

'Mum?' he called after her. 'Who's Nick?'

Alex stopped dead in her tracks, remembering to plaster a bright smile on her face as she wheeled around. 'Why do—' She stopped and felt the smile slide from her face.

Jason was crouched down where she'd been, holding a letter and looking at it quizzically. 'Was he your boyfriend or something?'

She took a step closer, heart in her mouth.

He is your father.

Her mind framed the words but her mouth refused to make the sounds. God, she needed time to work out how to tell him. 'Something like that. It was a long time ago.'

'Before I was born?'

She smiled, and without letting go of her cargo reached out a hand to muss his hair.

'Yes, before you were born.' She hesitated, aware that Jason was handing her the perfect opportunity to tell him all about his father and wondering where to start. 'He was a very special boyfriend, actually. I think you would have liked him.'

But Jason looked as if he'd already lost interest.

'Okay,' he said, shrugging. 'But don't ever think I'm going to write mushy stuff like that to some girl.' He screwed up his face and stuck out his tongue as he handed it to her. 'Totally gross,' he added, heading off back towards the kitchen, then turning. 'Oh, I forgot what I meant to ask you. Matt and Jack said I could go fishing with them by myself—if it's okay with you, that is?'

She smiled. 'Of course,' she said. 'And get that birthday party list worked out too—those invitations should go out soon.'

'Totally cool!' he said. 'I'll get onto it.'

She watched him happily trot off, confident that all was right in his world, and then she looked down at the letter, curious to see which letter her son had found. It was one of Nick's early letters, and straight away she caught a glimpse of the lines Jason must have been referring to.

Nick's words had made her swoon back then. Now they just made her stomach roll with a sense of foreboding she couldn't shake.

CHAPTER SIX

ALEX headed into the office on Monday morning firing on all cylinders. All Sunday, whether doing the housework, kicking a ball around with Jason in the nearby park or catching up on study, she'd been planning exactly what she'd say to Nick and how she'd tell him of their son.

She'd thought of everything. Every line of dialogue, every possible response from him. She had them all covered. She was prepared for every contingency.

Alex took a deep breath as she opened the door. It wasn't going to be easy, certainly, but nothing was going to stop her today from telling Nick the facts of his Australian legacy. The first opportunity she had, she was going to shut herself in his office and explain everything.

She swallowed, her throat suddenly dry at the thought of being shut in an office—*alone*—with Nick. Already her heart had kicked up a beat. Maybe that wasn't such a good idea. Maybe better to take him for coffee in the outdoor café downstairs—find a quiet table. At least it would be public. At least he couldn't back her into a corner there.

After that it would be up to him—if he wanted to

meet Jason she'd speak to him and arrange it. If he refused to acknowledge their boy then so be it. But at least she would have done what she needed to do.

He was there, sitting in what had used to be Aristos's spacious office, when she arrived. The Venetian blinds on the glass walls of his office were slatted open and she knew instinctively, without looking in, that he had noticed her arrival and was watching her.

'Alexandra.' His rich Mediterranean accent confirmed it as it flowed around her from the office. 'Good morning.'

Alex paused outside his open door and looked in. He gazed back from his position behind the wide expanse of timber desk. A small man could get lost behind that desk. Not Nick. The table complemented his dimensions, extending the range of his power and influence. This was a man who knew how to rule. This was a man born to power.

Alex suppressed the burn in her throat. Despite all his apparent strength, there was no time like the present. She dipped her head in acknowledgement, unable to smile.

'Morning,' she said briefly, knowing there was little good about it. She took a small step into his office. 'I need to talk to you. Are you free for the next few minutes?'

'Come in,' he said, pen poised over the documents he'd been signing. 'I need to speak to you today too. I won't be here tomorrow.'

He was leaving. Emotion crashed through her in waves—delight, disappointment and, overwhelmingly, relief. Gone would be the pressure of his everyday presence in the office. Gone would be the memories he brought to life by his touch. Gone would be the need to tell him about Jason…

'You're leaving? Going back to Greece?'

He put the pen down and looked up at her. A bare smile touched his lips. 'You would like that, would you not? For me to return to Greece? To relegate me to the past once more?'

She gulped—his words were far too close to the truth.

'Sorry to disappoint you. I'll be away only a week or so. I think it's time I saw the rest of the Xenophon properties before I make any long-term decisions. How many are there scattered around Australia— twelve or thirteen?'

'Fourteen, all up. If you count the shopping centre in Perth the company has just settled on.'

'Ah, fourteen.' He thought a second. 'Maybe a little longer than a week. I will spend some time in each city, talking to the property managers. I thought Sofia would come with me, but she wants to stay. She has a project she needs your help with.'

She nodded with a touch of resignation, more than used to assisting Sofia with her 'projects'. Past experience told her she'd be doing more of the actual project work herself, rather than merely assisting.

'And Alexandra…?'

His voice had dropped down a level, taken on a more intimate tone, and now he leaned closer, resting his forearms on the desk, hands clasped.

Her dry throat scratched out a shaky response. 'Yes?'

'Look after her for me while I'm gone. Make sure she has everything she needs.'

'Of course,' she said, her voice little more than a whisper. 'Consider it done.'

'Good.' He nodded, unclasped his fingers and stretched back in his chair. 'Now, what did you want to see me about?'

'Oh…' *Where to from here?* If Nick was only going to be away a few days there was no excuse for not telling him the truth about his son right now. And the separation might give him time to get used to the idea. Maybe there was a chance he might like to meet Jason when he got back, before his birthday. Give them time to get to know each other, if that was what they both wanted.

She hesitated. 'It's kind of private.'

Nick's eyebrows rose. 'You want to close the door?'

She shook her head. Even with the blinds open she didn't want to be trapped in that office with Nick, to have to tell him across that wide plain of a desk. He looked far too powerful, too strong.

'No, not here. How about in the courtyard? We'll get a coffee.'

His eyes narrowed a fraction, as if were mentally

assessing her response, and his lips curled up a tad. 'As you wish. Put down your things. I just have one phone call to make and then I'll expect you.'

Alex moved to her office, relieved herself of her laptop and briefcase and took a few calming breaths. There—she was committed. Tilly was right, she could do this.

She picked up her wallet. She'd pay her way. She'd owe Nick nothing.

She had turned to leave the office when Sofia sprang through the door and shut it behind her. She was grinning widely, her lips a bright pink slash across her impeccably made-up face.

'Alex, I need your help.'

Alex's spirits slumped. *Please, not now,* she thought. Not now, when I'm all psyched up for meeting Nick. For *telling* Nick.

'Can it wait a few minutes, Sofia? I have to talk to Nick. He's expecting me.'

She moved to go past, but Sofia threw out her arms, blocking her way. Alex caught a blast of the heavy sandalwood scent Sofia used so liberally.

'No. That can wait. This is too important.'

'I have a meeting…' Alex said, pointedly looking down at her watch.

'Notice anything?' Sofia invited, ignoring her protest.

Alex took a calming breath while her mind searched for whatever it was that was supposedly so apparent. Then it hit her. The blue stretch trousersuit fitted Sofia like a glove.

'Of course—your new suit. Lovely.' It should have registered earlier. Since that conversation last week Sofia had produced an entire new wardrobe. She'd worn something new, and blue, every day.

'No, silly.' She waggled her fingers, still out-stretched. 'Notice anything else?'

Alex's eyes followed the gesture. 'No, I—' *Then she saw it.* The diamond was almost as big as Ayers Rock—or so it seemed as every tiny facet dazzled with reflected light in its brilliance. She swallowed. 'Wow. That really is something.'

Sofia theatrically dropped her arms down so that her left hand sat uppermost in her other. She gazed down at the ring, admiring the play of reflected light.

'Thank you. Nick and I will be married as soon as possible.'

Alex's world lurched. *Nick?* It took too much energy to remain standing while her brain tried to process the information. She collapsed into her chair before her knees gave out completely.

'And that's why I need your help. There's so much to do, and I can't bother Nick with it all, with him going away—so will you help me organise the wedding?'

Nick! Getting married! *To Sofia?*

The girl was staring at her expectantly, the illumination of her new engagement bright in her eyes.

'Well…congratulations.' The word came out in a

rush as Alex struggled to make sense of her splintered thoughts. Organise Sofia's wedding? *How?* How would she cope with finding Sofia the perfect flowers, the perfect gown, only to send her down the aisle with the man she'd once dreamed of marrying herself?

'Will you? You know I've got no one else to help,' she pleaded, her head tilted to one side. 'Not any more, anyway.' Suddenly the eyes that a moment ago had been clear and bright misted over, and dampness clung thickly in her long mascaraed lashes.

The change in the girl's mood was instantaneous, and Alex realised how close to the edge Sofia was treading. Her brightness was only a thin veneer, ready to shatter any time and reveal the grieving girl beneath.

She scrabbled to find a gentle response, something that wouldn't hurt Sofia, but could somehow let her back out. 'I'd love to help,' she said, 'but what of my work? There's so much involved in planning a wedding, especially if there's not much time.'

'Nick's taken care of all that. He said he's bringing out his own accountant from Greece, so you should have time to help me.'

Ice flushed through Alex's veins. So that was the plan. This was Sofia's special project. He was keeping her on to help Sofia organise her wedding. What had he asked?

'Look after her for me while I'm gone. Make sure she has everything she needs.'

He was marrying Sofia. He'd asked Alex to be his

mistress for the duration of his stay and then turned
around and calmly offered marriage to someone else.
Yet still he expected her to help with the wedding
plans. What kind of man had he become? Certainly
not one she wanted to share her bed with, let alone
her son.

Alex thought of her mission, so fixed in her mind
just a short while ago.

How was she supposed to tell him now? Everything
had changed. Now there wasn't just Nick and Jason
to consider. Now Sofia had entered the equation.
Telling Nick would just create one whole new set of
problems, especially coming so soon after his engagement.

'He has to be told.'

Tilly's words battled their way uppermost in her
mind and Alex bit down on her lip, knowing that none
of her preceding thoughts counted for anything in the
end. No matter what she personally thought of the
man, no matter who he was now marrying, she still
had to tell him. She could find excuses for ever. But
it didn't change the underlying truth that he had a
right to know.

'It'll be fun—you'll see.'

She looked up at Sofia, so full of hope, so brimming with excitement and yet so perilously close to
despair, and she felt awful. She was being selfish.
After the tragedy of the past few weeks Sofia had a
right to be happy. Even if Alex couldn't imagine any-

thing less fun, there was at least one way she could help the girl.

'I'm not sure I'd be the best person for the job,' she began, 'but I know a great wedding planner who might be able to help. Do you want me to call her?'

Sofia jumped up and down, clapping her hands, her earlier near breakdown forgotten. 'Cool! I want to get started right away. Can you organise an appointment for me today? Any time—let me know. Only there's so much to do.'

'Sure. I'll give her a call.'

Behind Sofia, Nick opened the door. 'We had a meeting, remember?'

His words sounded short, and his face was dark, as though she'd kept him waiting purposely. Then he saw Sofia and Alex witnessed his face relax, the scowl replaced with a smile as he turned his attention to her.

'I didn't realise you were back in the office. Is everything all right?' He took Sofia's hand and pulled her closer as he leaned down towards her. Sofia raised her face, her beaming love-filled face full of hope and optimism for the future, and Alex saw him smile back, and then she just couldn't watch any more.

She didn't have to look. It was obvious what came next. He was kissing her. He was kissing his future bride—*right in front of her.*

She had to hand it to him. He was one fast operator. He obviously had no intention of waiting six months for his inheritance. He'd earn his half-share right now, by marrying Sofia. And she was more than happy to go along with it.

Alex took a deep breath, trying to regain some perspective. What was her problem? What Nick and Sofia decided was their business. It shouldn't matter. It didn't matter. *So why did it feel so wrong?*

She sensed the couple move apart. 'We've just been discussing my project,' said Sofia, sounding more than a little breathless. 'She's agreed to help me with a few things, just like you promised, but she's all yours now. Don't keep her long, though. She's got a lot to do today.' Sofia winked back over her shoulder on her way out.

Alex picked up her wallet and mobile phone, purposely avoiding Nick's dark eyes and whatever they might tell her. 'Let's go.'

He fell into stride alongside her for the short walk to the café and Alex was choked by his presence. She should congratulate him, but the words wouldn't come, couldn't squeeze past the lump in her chest. *Did he need to be so close?* She could feel the heat emanating from him, could catch a hint of his cologne, and she wondered if it was such a good idea to leave the office after all. When their hands brushed Alex started, the zap as effective as any electric fence.

She covered the movement by folding her arms over her chest, hugging her wallet as she concentrated on keep her breathing calm. *Breathe in. Breathe out.*

Whatever had happened between them was in the past. Now he was getting married. He shouldn't affect her. She wouldn't let him affect her. Not if she was going to be able to tell him the truth. And she would.

They ordered their coffee and chose a table under the shade of a vine-covered pergola, a discreet distance from the other customers. Nick held out a chair and dutifully waited while she sat down. His hands seem to linger for ever on the back of the chair and his breath stirred the loose ends of the twist of hair she had pinned up that morning, sending warm tingles through her skin.

The next moment he had touched the clip holding the coil in place. 'What would happen if this came out?' His warm breath touched her neck, curling into her senses.

Alex's breath stuck as he toyed gently with the edge of the clip. 'My hair would fall down.' She ducked her head a fraction and one hand went up to reassure herself that the style was holding—only to have her hand snared by his.

He moved around the table and sat alongside without letting go. 'I should very much enjoy watching that,' he said, with a look that made her breath catch in her throat.

Alex looked into his dark eyes and not for the first time wished he didn't look quite so damned sexy. Wished he didn't make her feel so uncomfortable— so hot. Wished he wasn't marrying Sofia.

Crazy. She had to stop thinking like that. Who Nick married was not up to her. It shouldn't matter. She should be happy for both of them. And she would be—starting right now. She licked her lips, slipping her hand out of his and tucking it safely away with her other, deep in her lap.

'Sofia is very excited today.' She paused, still struggling to come out with 'that' word. 'I…I guess I should congratulate you. It's lovely to see her so happy after all she's been through.'

His eyes stayed on her, narrowing slightly, while his head tilted a fraction. 'She's a beautiful girl who deserves the best. I want her to be happy…'

Their coffee arrived. Alex, grateful for the interruption, stirred a spoonful of sugar she didn't need into her cappuccino, her spoon making lazy circles in the froth as her mind formed crazy, jagged spikes.

Of course Sofia was beautiful. And she deserved to be happy. But hearing him say those things about someone else, *his fiancée*, rubbed her nerve endings raw.

'So,' he said, after taking a sip of his long black coffee, 'here we are, sharing coffee. What is this private matter that you couldn't tell me in the office?'

Her heartbeat racing, she toyed with the froth on her coffee with her spoon, trying to form the words. 'Nick, I know we got off on the wrong foot, but I have to tell you something…'

He smiled again, and pushed back against his chair. The fine cotton of his shirt did nothing to hide the play of muscle just below the surface and Alex drank in the view. Everything about Nick shouted man, from his rugged olive-skinned jawline to the way his trousers fitted across his muscle-tight thighs. She looked up to realise he was watching her, obviously amused by her interest, and even more than that. He seemed to be *enjoying* her interest.

Cheeks flushed with heat, she pressed on.

'I have certain responsibilities that I need to discuss with you—that you should be aware of.'

He smiled again, wider, with one side tilted up, and he was nodding. It threw her. He didn't look curious or concerned. He looked somehow *satisfied*.

'I knew you would have a change of heart,' he cut in. 'But don't worry. I have taken that into account. You were right to want this meeting outside the office. It's much more discreet.'

Confusion clouded her mind. 'Sorry? I'm not with you.'

'We can't meet at your house, I realise, with your "responsibilities".' He moved closer to her, bending his head towards hers. 'I would suggest my apartment, but Sofia has a tendency to drop in whenever she feels like it and I don't want to upset her. I will arrange another apartment for us.'

Alex's eyes rounded as he continued with his plans. *He had to be kidding!* 'No,' she said, interrupting his flow. 'No apartment.'

He brushed aside her protest with a wave of his hand. 'It's more discreet. We can both have a key—'

'*No apartment!* I told you I won't sleep with you. What makes you think I'd change my mind?'

Especially now. Now that she'd been asked to arrange Sofia's wedding. Sofia and Nick's wedding. What kind of man was he, that he could coolly take a mistress while plans for his wedding to another woman were made? Poor Sofia. Did she have any idea what she was letting herself in for? Thinking of the girl just hardened her resolve.

'I won't change my mind.'

'Oh, you'll change your mind,' he said, in a whisper that sounded disturbingly like a threat. 'I'll make it worth your while. You won't have to scratch along on the pitiful wage Aristos paid you.'

She pushed back her chair and stood. '*Nothing* you can offer would make it worthwhile. What's happened to you, Nick, that you can be so callous and hard? When did you stop feeling?'

She picked up her things from the table and moved away, but already he was standing in front of her and blocking her exit.

'Before you go…' he said, leaning closer. He took her shoulder with one hand, and even though she held herself rigid she felt herself being drawn closer to him. His face dipped closer to hers, and for one insane moment she thought he was going to kiss her. She looked up as his face grew nearer, his eyes swirling with the unknown, and her lips parted of their own accord.

Then he gently brushed her upper lip with one finger, leaving her completely and utterly breathless.

'You had chocolate on your lip,' he said, before lifting the finger to his mouth and licking it clean.

For a moment she was too shocked to respond. For one thing the gesture had been completely unnecessary. For another it had been way too intimate. But the worst of it was that she felt cheated.

Because for some insane reason she had found herself wanting that kiss. And it hadn't happened.

'Thank you,' she forced herself to say through gritted teeth, her voice scratchy. Breaking eye contact, and trying to pretend that having cappuccino foam practically licked off her lip was an everyday occurrence, she headed resolutely for the office.

'The pleasure was all mine,' she heard Nick mutter a few paces behind her.

The phone was ringing when she got back to her office.

'So how did it go?' asked Tilly.

'It didn't.'

'You mean you didn't tell him?'

'I couldn't.'

'You chickened out?' Tilly's tone was damning.

'I tried to tell him but he wasn't listening. And things have changed.'

'What's changed?'

'He's marrying Sofia.'

A pause. 'Are you sure?'

'Tilly, he's bought her a diamond the size of Uluru and they've both asked me to help with the wedding. How much more evidence do I need?'

'Oh.' Alex could hear the sound of Tilly sitting down. 'Are you okay about it?'

Alex scoffed. 'Why should it matter? Nick means nothing to me now.'

Liar! Even as she said the words it felt as if someone was twisting a knife inside her. And yet it shouldn't matter, so why the hell did she feel so bad?

'I guess that does complicate things. But he still—'

Alex cut her off, knowing full well what was coming. 'Yeah, I know. I just couldn't do it on top of everything else. Not today.' *Not after he'd offered to set me up in an apartment for sex whenever he felt like it.* She glanced at her watch. 'Listen, sis, I need your help. I can't do this wedding planning thing. I don't have the first idea of how to go about planning a wedding, let alone the extravaganza Sofia will expect—besides which, I have far too much work on my plate already. So I recommended you. Can you do it?'

'So…you're not actually okay about it?'

Alex sighed. 'Look, it's complicated. Let's leave it at that. Now, do you want this job or not?'

Tilly rang off once they'd worked out a time for Sofia to drop by, and Alex worked out that she had better deal with the bank and transfer some money pronto. Sofia's credit card had maxed out—no mean feat, given the gold-plated limit. The new blue wardrobe had obviously taken its toll. She authorised a transfer to ensure there was sufficient credit to cover the inevitable imminent shopping spree and went in search of the blushing bride-to-be.

CHAPTER SEVEN

TIME, like Alex's peace of mind, was wearing thin. It had been a quiet couple of weeks. Tilly had kept Sofia so busy, organising the wedding of her dreams, that she'd hardly been in the office. Nick had extended his trip away, as expected. He was due back tomorrow, in time to collect Dimitri—who was arriving from Athens—from the airport.

Everything was ready. The invoices were up to date. The bank statements reconciled. The management reports were prepared—a neat stack of facts and figures to greet the new administrator, who would need all of this to evaluate the Xenophon Group's operations.

She'd achieved a lot in just a few days—achieved all that she'd set out to do and more. But there was no rush of satisfaction at having met her self-imposed targets. No spring in her step at having smoothed the chaos that had been the office, since Aristos's death, into order and control.

Nick was coming back tomorrow. Somehow the anticipation of that—the dread of that—overpowered everything else.

But that was tomorrow.

She glanced at her watch. It was late, and it was

time she left if she wasn't going to be late picking up Jason from after-school care.

Then she remembered. Sofia had left the copy for her engagement notice for the weekend papers on her desk, wanting it to be faxed to the newspaper today. She made a quick call to the newspaper, checked it wasn't too late, and started keying in the number in the backroom fax. The front office door swung open and clicked shut.

'I'll be right with you,' she called down the hall-way, wondering why a courier would be delivering this late in the day.

The fax machine beeped its way through the number and started churning through the page. Satisfied that the copy would make it to the newspaper desk, as promised, Alex turned—only to collide with solid man, solid heat.

'Nick!' she said, bouncing breathlessly off his chest as his hands shot out to steady her. 'I didn't hear you.'

Nick held onto her shoulders, even though she was in no danger of falling now.

'We didn't expect you until tomorrow. Sofia will be pleased.'

He hesitated a second. 'And are you pleased, Alexandra?'

His face was close, the late afternoon stubble on his skin lending a dark, threatening shadow to his jaw. He smelt of coffee, of airline whisky, and man. Pure, unadulterated testosterone. It assailed her senses. It permeated her skin through his touch on her shoulders. It tickled her nose and warmed her lungs, her chest, her body.

She swallowed. 'How did the trip go?'

'You haven't answered my question. Are you pleased I'm back?'

His eyes glinted, challenging her as his words had done a moment before. It made her kick up her chin.

'No. I mean, yes. I mean—'

His eyes lit up and his lips curled. 'Yes *and* no? Some good, some not so good. Tell me how this can be.'

Alex paused. She hadn't meant to be so honest. But how to respond? She gulped. 'Yes, because it's good you're back safely.' *Chicken.* 'And no, because you seem to enjoy making my life difficult.' At least that bit was true.

'I don't mean to make your life difficult. I think you do that yourself.'

'What?' she said, trying unsuccessfully to shrug out of his hands. 'How do you figure that?'

'Because I know what your answer really means.' Alex stilled her struggles. All of a sudden his grip noticeably gentled; now he was stroking languid lines along to her neck. After the strain of a long day assembling reports, the massaging effect was heaven. Her head dipped involuntarily towards his stroking touch.

'You are scared of me. Your head tells you I shouldn't be here, while at the same time your body reaches out for me.'

Her head snapped up.

'Rubbish. I—'

His massage grew more firm, retaining her within his grasp. 'And that's how you make your life more difficult. By denying yourself the pleasure you know you will find with me.'

His arms tightened around her as he moved closer, cupping her head with his hands.

'And there is no doubt you will find pleasure with me.'

She gazed up at him and knew he was right. She was battling the demon of desire and it was sapping her of all her strength. Yes, she would find pleasure with him. Of that there was no doubt. But it was a battle she had to fight. A battle she had to win.

Only now, with his face descending towards hers, passion flaring in those deep, dark eyes as his hands continued to mould her to him, it was hard to remember why.

Her breasts felt him first, her nipples crushing to his chest with a burning need to get closer, ever closer. She let herself be gathered tight in his embrace, pressing herself against the long, strong length of his body, watching him dip his head, slant his lips across hers. They shared a breath between them, shared the air that gave them both life but still wasn't enough to sustain their need.

His lips grazed hers, the barest touch, the hint of recollection strong and hypnotic, and then something like a groan, his need given voice, emanated from deep in his throat and his mouth meshed with hers at last. She responded in kind, parting her lips willingly as his urged her to, his taste in her mouth and his breath taking hers away. His hands splayed at her neck, down her back, sculpting her body as they travelled her length.

For a moment his lips left hers to trail kisses down her neck, and she looked heavenwards, gratefully gasping in much needed oxygen, before they sought her mouth once more and she welcomed him back, her hand raking through his hair. He was so much the same, this man she'd known before. So much the same and yet so different. So much more a man. So much more…

The years melted away under the onslaught of his kisses, banished by a desire that had never changed, never diminished. His touch on her body was electric. Nerve cells kicked into life at his touch, skin goosebumped and tingled.

All over her feelings were awakening at his touch—exquisite torture as still it was not enough. His lips and tongue duelled with hers while his hands were everywhere—her hair, her neck, her back, her thigh.

Alex gasped as his hand slipped under her raised skirt and slid around to capture her behind. He responded by kissing her deeper, urging her closer against his obvious hardness.

'Alexandra,' he murmured, nuzzling her ear, 'I want you.'

His words fed her own need, even as something inside told this was wrong. A kiss was going too far. And this was way beyond a kiss.

He steered her back towards the desk, jamming her hard against it as his hand lifted the skirt on the other side.

'No,' she whispered, her voice husky and raw. She pulled back, leaning over the desk, away from him, but he only took it as an opportunity for his hand to snare her breast. A sharp intake of air filled her lungs.

'No! Don't, Nick. This shouldn't be happening.'

He pulled back, but only for a moment. 'We've been through all that. This is exactly what *should* be happening.' He leaned closer, aiming for her lips once more. 'It's time to stop fighting it.'

Breath hissed through Alex's clenched teeth.

'This is wrong!'

He moved to kiss her and she swung her head away so his lips collided with her cheek.

'Stop playing games.' His tone was brusque, annoyed, and his hands moved from her thighs to restrain her arms. 'You want this as much as I do.'

She turned her face back to his, painfully aware that her breath was coming in choppy bursts and trying to keep her voice level in spite of it. 'And what does Sofia want? Doesn't that matter too?'

'This doesn't concern her. This is between you and me.'

The anger his words created welled up inside her, giving her a strength she hadn't realised she owned.

She managed to free one hand, pulled it back and cracked it solidly against his cheek.

He recoiled, looking almost amused—except for his eyes. They glinted at her, dark and menacing. She'd taken him by surprise, that much was sure, and he didn't like it.

'How can you say that,' she demanded, 'when your engagement is to be announced in two days?'

Beside her the fax machine beeped into life, snagging Alex's attention. The brief notice spat out. A confirmation.

The *Sydney Daily* had received the announcement she had sent through just minutes before. The day after tomorrow Sofia and Nick's engagement would be official.

For the first time Nick relaxed his hold and leaned back.

'What did you say?' He spun away suddenly, both hands raking through his hair. Alex felt his departure as a sudden absence of heat but couldn't afford to mourn the loss. She took a deep, shuddering breath.

'And this is how you behave.'

She fled to her office to snatch up her things. She was leaving—now! She threw her parting words over her shoulder as she walked out.

'I'm sorry, Nick. Contract or not, I'm not staying in this place another second.'

CHAPTER EIGHT

HE SLOWED the Mercedes Sports to a crawl and came to a halt alongside number nineteen. This was definitely the place. That was her small car there, parked in the narrow driveway.

But who owned the red two-door nestled in close behind? She'd said she didn't have a partner. His gut clenched at the prospect she might have lied to him.

She'd said she had 'responsibilities'. Was that what she'd been trying to tell him at the café—that she had a relationship, that she had a boyfriend she'd been reluctant to admit to?

He watched the house for a few minutes, his window wound down, the light morning breeze puffing through the opening. You could smell the sea from here. Smell it but not see it. She hadn't bought a place right on the sea. Surprising after her love affair with the sea in Crete. She'd loved its deep, bright blue against the stark white of sand or the rubble of rock. Surely she could have found something closer than this? Or was this all she was able to afford?

He looked at the ageing cottage again—there wasn't a lot to it: a single-fronted older style place, built of stone, with flaking wooden fretwork around the small verandah out front, and all topped by a typical red Sydney roof in obvious need of repair. There wasn't much garden—a palm in a pot and a couple of old rose bushes—although a view down the side hinted at the promise of a bigger back garden behind.

Movement at the front door snared his attention. Someone came out—a woman. It had been a long time but still he recognised her. A taller and blonder version of Alexandra. She must be the wedding planner. He watched her wave back towards the house and then turn for her car. The front door closed and the woman made her way to the sporty hatch, curled herself inside and reversed out.

Nick breathed again, waited until the vehicle moved away down the road, eased himself out of the car and approached the front door.

He rang the bell. Nothing seemed to happen for a moment or two. He pushed the button again.

'Okay,' came Alex's voice from inside. 'I'm coming.'

She pulled the door open, 'What did you—?' the words stalled on her lips as her blue eyes widened and rose up to meet his '—lose?'

'My fiancée.'

She stood at the door, wearing the type of clothes he hadn't seen her in since Crete—jeans and a knitted top that fitted her like a second skin, showing off every curve that had been hidden under her work suits. All of a sudden he realised why women weren't supposed to wear jeans to the office. It would be far, far too distracting.

She looked up at him, her lips apart and questioning, and he saw something like a shudder move through her. 'What?' Then she appeared to collect herself, but, still with confusion swirling in her expression, shook her head. 'No, Sofia's not here.'

Nick shook his own head slowly. 'I'm not looking for Sofia.'

Her eyes, once wide and questioning, now pulled tight into a taut frown. 'Then what did you mean?'

He waited a second, tongue poised at his lips as a motorbike roared down the street behind him, then another, yanking his gaze around.

It was next to impossible to be heard over the racket.

'Are you going to invite me in, or do we have to try to discuss this on your doorstep?'

She frowned as her eyes followed the bikes powering down the narrow street. 'I'm sorry about that. The Simpsons from number fifty-two. They're into motorbikes.' She shrugged, as if that explained everything, and then led the way inside.

The living room was not large, just as he had anticipated from his view of the outside, yet still it held a warmth that seemed to wrap itself around him—worn but comfortable chairs; a thin, almost threadbare rug in muted shades; smiling faces peering out at him from the photographs adorning nearly every horizontal surface. Smiling faces of a young boy growing up.

He stopped on impulse, picking one up.

She turned, sensing his stillness, saw what he held in his hands and held her breath.

Time stood still. Would he be able to tell, just from a photograph?

Finally he looked up, his forehead creased. 'Your son?'

She nodded weakly, her mouth dry. *Our son.* 'Jason,' she finally managed, trying to get moisture to her lips so she could say more…

'Good-looking boy,' he said with a nod. 'How could his father do this to you? Leave you with his son all alone? Why would a father not want a son like this? What kind of man is he?'

She swallowed, strangely let down that he hadn't made the connection and that still the onus remained firmly on her to tell him. 'He didn't mean to. It wasn't really his fault.'

His eyebrows drew together in a deep scowl. 'He left you alone. And yet you defend him. Did you love him that much?'

With all her soul. Tears pricked at the corners of her eyes and she turned her head away. It seemed almost laughable now, given the way he'd treated her since his arrival, given the man he'd become. 'I once thought I did.'

'Then don't you hate him for what he's done?'

She looked over at him imploringly and indicated the photo still in his hand. 'How could I ever hate him? Look what he's given me. I still have Jason. At least I have him. I have that much.'

He moved suddenly, thumping the photograph back onto the mantel, and she sensed she'd said the wrong thing—even though she'd spoken only the truth—something had angered him.

She dragged in a deep breath. 'Why are you here?' she asked, clasping her arms with her hands. Then, in case he was here to change her mind, added, 'Because you know I'm not coming back to the Xenophon Group.'

'I assumed that you would say that—even if I told you what Dimitri said.'

Her head tilted one side, curiosity getting the better of her. 'Why? What did he say?'

'He said he couldn't understand why I'd brought him out here when things were being managed so well.'

'He did?'

He nodded. 'There are a few small changes Dimitri would recommend. But on the whole he is happy with the operation and how it has been run.'

Alex digested his words, feeling unexpected pride in the job she'd left. It was worth something that her work had been appreciated, even if not by Nick himself.

'So, then, if it's not to lure me back to the company, why are you here?'

He looked around. 'Where is the boy?'

'Jason's not home. He's gone fishing with some friends.' He seemed to visibly relax, at least a fraction, as if he was no longer concerned about being interrupted by a child. She was sure he wasn't half as relieved as she was. If Nick had dropped by when Jason was home—she shuddered to think about it. She was having enough trouble trying to tell Nick about their son. There was no way she could handle revealing the truth to the two of them together.

'He won't be home for a while,' she prompted when he still just gazed out of the window, not comfortable about telling him that Jason was away for the weekend, but wanting to say something that might prompt him to speak and reveal the reason for his visit.

He turned towards her and she was struck by the sheer force of his presence. Black jeans and a casual shirt did nothing to lessen the impact of his power. It was there. All around him. He carried it like people carried the air in their lungs. He carried it like a birthright.

'I'm not marrying Sofia.'

Alex was grateful for the arm of the chair alongside. It gave her something to cling to. Something welcomingly concrete.

He wasn't getting married. Part of her wanted to jump up and shout that it had been clear from the start that Sofia was never right for him, while another part of her wondered why she should feel so vindicated by the announcement.

But why would he come here to let her know? Did he think it mattered? Unless Nick simply assumed she was the perfect person to cancel the wedding plans for him because her sister was the planner.

'Hold on,' she said. 'What about the notice in the paper today?' She managed the few steps to the table, where the paper lay open at the employment section, checked on the front page for the index to notices and flicked through. 'I placed the notice myself.'

'Did you see the announcement?'

She kept her eyes on the paper. 'No, not yet. I...' In truth she hadn't looked beyond the employment pages. Why confirm what she knew? She had to think about her own future now. Not someone else's.

'I can't find it,' she said, her eyes skimming the engagements section.

'It's not there. I cancelled it.'

'Why? What happened?'

'Simple,' he said. 'I'm not getting married.'

'Then why get engaged in the first place?' she argued, rubbing her forehead with her fingers, feeling annoyed for both Sofia—who'd no doubt be devastated—and for her sister, who'd spent so long planning for the upcoming nuptials. 'Why buy her that ring?'

'I never bought that ring.'

'But...' Alex was about to protest until she recalled that phone call she'd had to make to the bank. The one clearing Sofia's credit card account of an amount hugely over her five-figure limit.

'*Sofia* bought it?'

He shrugged and moved a little closer to the table,

picking up and investigating her bits and pieces along the way. 'I can only presume. Seeing I had nothing to do with it.'

'But you were getting married. All those plans...'

His breath was expelled in one fast, furious motion and he put down the clay kangaroo Jason had crafted in school with a decided thump. Alex started at the sound, relieved the artwork had survived, and then her eyes caught his and she realised there was no such thing as relief when those eyes were on her—not with the way they turned on a switch deep inside, like a kettle, so that her emotions could go from millpond-calm to bubbling turmoil in less than a minute.

'She said she was doing market research into the bridal industry.' He laughed a short, bitter laugh as he raised his eyes to the ceiling. 'I thought she was looking at our tenant mix, to see if we were covering all the bases. It seems she had other ideas.'

'Then you were never getting married? Never even engaged?'

His dark eyes locked back on hers and tripped her internal switch again. 'Never.'

A deep breath filled her lungs. 'Sofia was so sure...'

She'd been so sure! Sofia was marrying Nick. Yet suddenly everything had changed.

He frowned and turned his gaze outside once more. 'Sofia is Aristos's daughter through and through. She wants exactly what her father wanted for her—marriage to someone he approved of, and preferably someone with links to the family. She assumed I was that person and somehow that helped to ease her grief.'

'But I congratulated you. You told me...' She thought about his words. He wanted Sofia to be happy. He wanted her to have the best. But not once had he said he was going to marry her. She'd taken Sofia's fantasy and turned it into her own reality.

Nick just shook his head. 'She's all alone. I know what that's like. She needs looking after and I intend to get her help in coming to terms with her father's death. But even if I was interested spending my life with Sofia, I'm the least qualified person to build any sort of family with.'

She couldn't let his last statement lie. He'd said the words as a cold statement of fact, without a hint of self-pity. It was clear he really believed it, and Alex couldn't help but bridge the few steps between them. 'Nick, I'm sure that's not true.'

Her hand found his bare forearm, intending to console, but the second she made contact any altruistic intention flew from her head. His flesh was rock-firm beneath her touch, yet strangely at odds with the softer, springier coating of hair. Her fingers were fascinated by the contrast. Hard and yet soft. Different parts of the same thing. Was that how Nick himself was? Different parts of the same thing? Only in Nick's case he seemed to be harder on the outside, where it showed to the world. Hard and decisive and unforgiving.

Did he have a softer inside lurking below that harsh public exterior, hidden deep below?

She wanted to believe so.

'It doesn't matter,' he said, his brow knotting as he gazed down at her hand. 'I just came to tell you that I'm leaving. I'm going home to Greece, and for good now that Dimitri is here to manage the operation. It was a long shot, but I just wanted you to know that if you wanted your old job back—'

She pulled her arm away.

'My job? After all you've done to ensure it goes to someone else? What is this, some last-ditch attempt to buy me now that Sofia doesn't stand in the way?'

Without taking a step it felt he was closer. Heat emanated from him and his eyes focused on hers until even the air between them dissolved. 'I don't need to buy you.'

Breath rushed through her. He was too close, too threatening, too dangerous. But he she couldn't let him get away with that. She had to ask. She swallowed, kicking her chin up a notch.

'What makes you so sure of yourself?'

In a breath he was there, right next to her, filling her body with heat simply by his proximity. He looked down at her, making her skin tingle with just his gaze, his eyes certain and his words just as sure. 'Because there's never been any question. You have always been mine.'

Her intake of breath was arrested by his lips, his mouth slanting over hers as his arms surrounded her and gathered her into his chest. Everywhere they made contact her body felt the heat, responded to it as every cell swelled and firmed and sought to get even closer to him. His hands swept her back as his mouth magicked hers, weaving a spell of want and need.

For a moment she thought of arguing the point. But only for a moment. The way her body responded he'd know in an instant she was lying. She had always been his. There'd never been another she'd even looked at. She had never wanted anyone else. In nine years there had been only one man who had haunted her dreams and filled her nights with want. Only the man holding her now. Only Nick. Only ever Nick.

It was impossible not to respond, not to match his passion with her own pent-up desire. He wasn't marrying Sofia! Her heart sang with the knowledge, though there was no time to analyse why. Not with Nick's taste in her mouth, his breath merged with hers and his touch set her body alight.

Her hand found a gap between shirt and jeans and her fingers immediately took advantage, seeking the skin beneath. A deep sound issued from his throat as she found the hot flesh beneath and found what she was looking for—skin-to-skin contact. She forced the shirt higher, until both her hands could roam his back, feeling the tight play of muscles as his arms moved over her.

'Today we will make love.' His voice was a husky

whisper against her ear, so that she felt it more as vibration than as sound.

She wasn't about to argue. His simple statement of fact was beyond argument. They both knew it. This time they would make love. A small tremor, filled with expectation and promise, moved through her.

His head pulled back a fraction from hers. His eyes were dark and smoky with desire. Desire for her. She saw the eyes of the young man on Crete all those years ago and breath caught in her throat. The eyes he'd turned on her back then were hers again.

And she knew in that instant that she still loved him. Totally, utterly, completely. She loved him and she'd never stopped loving him through all the years. It wasn't just her body that was Nick's. Her heart belonged to him too.

'Your boy—when is he due home?'

She swallowed, reluctant to break the mood but knowing that this secret between them had to be revealed. 'Nick, I have to tell you something. I—'

'When will he be home?'

'Tomorrow—he's gone camping overnight.'

She caught the gleam in his eye, the smile that rocked the corners of his mouth. He gently shook his head and shooshed her with a finger to her lips. 'We've both said too many words.' In one easy movement he lifted and swung her into his arms. 'Tell me tomorrow. Now it is time we made love.'

He kissed her again, and she kissed him back,

grateful that now nothing was going to stop their inevitable, inescapable date with destiny.

Today they would make love.

And tomorrow she would tell him about his son.

Still kissing her, he headed down the narrow side hallway. The kitchen waited at the end of the hall and two doors led off to the left in between. He paused at the first door and she shook her head under his lips. He continued to the next.

She pushed it open with her foot and he carried her inside the high-ceilinged room, decorated in Victorian shades and dominated by an old iron-framed double bed. She shuddered against him as she thought of the bed, of Nick with her, and he squeezed her tightly, as if sensing her nervousness.

Then he eased her down gently, so gently, as if she might break, in the centre of the bed and gazed deeply into her eyes, into her soul. 'I want to see you naked,' he said. 'I want to see your skin. But first...' He reached behind her head to prise open and slip out the clip holding her hair in its tight, twisted knot. With his other hand he shook the hair free, until it spilled around her shoulders in a wave of blonde foam.

He made a rough sound of approval, deep in his throat, held her face in his two hands and kissed her gently on the lips. 'And now to feel your skin.' He sat alongside her on the bed and eased her light knitted top over her head. He threw it to one side and stopped, riveted, his eyes hotly on her.

She sat there, his intense dark gaze upon her, recognising the appreciation and sheer desire therein. As if spellbound, he reached out a hand and touched her skin. Her breath tracked in sharply and he sighed as her chest swelled in response. Lightly his finger traced the line of her champagne lace bra, burning her skin as his fingers followed the strap down from her shoulders, circling each breast so gently she thought she would explode. He took his hand away and his knuckles brushed one nipple—instinctively her back arched in response and in a second both hands were gone. She knew just where a second later when she felt her bra relax, its rear clip manipulated open. A moment later her breasts felt the freedom of the air as he swept all trace of the bra away.

His following swift intake of air empowered her. He wanted her. Exposed to his appreciative gaze, her nipples hardened in the firm, goosebumped skin of her breasts. As much as she wanted his eyes to drink her in, her breasts craved the touch of his hand, his mouth.

She took one of his hands and held it against her. He smiled, squeezing his fingers around her flesh and following likewise with the other hand. He shifted his grip so that one hand supported her behind her back while he kissed her and eased her down flat on the bed. His kiss deepened, his hands once again exploring her breasts. It wasn't enough. Just as he wanted to look at her skin, to feel her skin, she needed that contact too. As his lips traced down the line of her neck she scrabbled with the buttons on his shirt.

In a final flurry the sides of his shirt flew apart and she pulled him down on her so that her skin met his. Her senses sizzled as their warm flesh meshed and merged. Everywhere they touched felt like paradise, and a whole lot of reason to go on. When he suddenly pushed her away she felt cold, a sense of abandonment. But in a second he'd discarded the shirt and his mouth was back, seeking out the flesh of her breast, taking her nipple in his mouth, rolling its tight bud around with his tongue and sucking with such gentle, even pressure that she felt the layers of her old life being stripped away, leaving only that which Nick had tasted before.

He caressed each nipple in turn, the warmth of his mouth rendering them harder and more insistent, sending shards of sensation down to the base of her deepest need.

And while his tongue went to work her own hands explored his body, stroking and massaging his shoulders, his ribs, his stomach—wherever they could reach.

She felt each sculpted dip between his ribs, felt the play of muscle under skin and the touch of his satiny olive skin. And still it wasn't enough. It wasn't enough to be close. It wasn't enough to touch.

For eight long years she had tried to shut this man out of her mind, tried to shut him out of her heart. But there was no denying the truth of how she felt.

Now her body prepared to welcome him back inside, where she wanted him, where she needed him more than anything else.

He eased down the zip of her jeans and peeled them down her legs, collecting her panties and flicking off her sandals in the same desperate movement. His hands glided down her legs, gentle in touch but electric in intensity. Everywhere he touched sparked and fused. Desire rippled through her as the inevitable nearness of their union struck home.

He kneeled over her and took a deep breath, one hand now skimming over the skin of her stomach. She flinched slightly, knowing she was different from that girl who'd made love to him as a teenager. Since then this body had stretched, had borne a child, and she knew more than anyone of the telltale, even if somewhat faded proof of that. How would he react to that?

'So beautiful, Alexandra. You are more beautiful than I remember.'

His words swelled her chest, bringing a smile to her mouth that was a mixture of pride and gratitude that he found her this way, that his eyes worshipped her. 'Make love to me,' she said, suddenly sitting up and stretching one hand out to him.

His actions spoke loud in response as, without taking his eyes from her, he unbuckled his belt and shucked off his jeans. And then he was naked, and it was her turn to catch her breath. All the dreams she'd had, all the nights she'd imagined Nick in her thoughts—they were nothing compared to the sight of the man who stood before her now.

She'd asked him to make love to her and only now did she realise what that entailed. She gulped down both wind and courage as she registered the sheer physical presence of him next to her. His abdomen, tight and muscular, the olive skin smooth and sheened, his hips, lean and strong, promising delivery of satisfaction—and beyond.

He reached out and took her hand. 'Alexandra,' he said, his voice husky, almost catching as he lowered himself down alongside her. He held her hand to his mouth and kissed the palm of her hand—a gesture so simple yet somehow so intimate that she was moved by the depth of feeling it inspired in her.

'Nick…' she said, before his lips found hers once more and there was no need for words of any kind. Their bodies spoke a language known only to them, his body wooing her with his strength and mastery, and her body responding to every subtle intonation and expression. His hands spoke of rediscovery, and her body sang with reawakening. His body spoke of his need, and hers answered it.

Pressure mounted within her until only one thing mattered and that was to have Nick fill her, to make the last nine years disappear in a blur of passion and desire. She clutched him, felt the slick sheen of his sweat at his lower back, and wished for him to fill her.

He kissed her and growled deep and low, pulling

away. 'One moment,' he said, and then he was back—and when she realised what he was doing she almost cried out with relief. He was protecting her. While she was touched by his consideration, there was much more immediate cause to celebrate. At last! Soon he would be inside her and this long, dragging ache inside her would be gone.

He positioned himself between her legs, his hands at her hips. Without thinking she raised them in greeting and he accepted her invitation, nudging gently at first, then more insistently, before finally driving home the full glorious length of him.

Both of them stopped for a second, as if in awe of the moment. Alex felt her eyes widen with shock and pleasure combined. The moment held such clarity and purpose, as if both had been waiting too long for this moment to arrive and it was here.

Slowly at first he started moving, withdrawing, teasing, before filling her once more with his next thrust.

Alex moved under him, pleasure mounting into delicious torture, and she looked for release. It came in his next surging thrust and her immediate world exploded, again and again, as he filled every space inside her, just as he filled her heart.

They rocked together, feeling the tremors diminish, their breathing subside, their sweat-slicked bodies at last gentling, and Alex knew there would only ever be one man for her. How she'd managed to try and ignore the fact for the last nine years she had no idea.

For now it was crystal-clear that there would never be room in her heart or her bed for any man other than Nick.

And he was leaving.

Breath stopped in her chest. He hadn't said when, just that he was going back to Greece. In a few days or a few hours he'd be gone, and she would have lost him to another hemisphere once again.

His hand pushed some hair from her eyes, and, surprised, she turned to meet Nick's dark eyes on her.

'You are thinking,' he said. 'Tell me what you are thinking of.'

She smiled. 'Just—thank you.' It was the truth too. She did owe him thanks—thanks for showing a gentler side of him, a side she'd thought lost completely under the bitter armour he'd built up around himself over the last few years, thanks for showing her that the man she'd thought lost was still there, deep down inside him.

His eyebrows and lips rose together, and his hand drew a line down the side of her face and down to her breast, circling the nipple.

'Thank you for asking me. Now it is my turn to ask you.' His hand traced down to her navel, again circling. In spite of its recent release, her body stirred in delicious response. 'Make love to me, Alexandra.'

She felt him harden alongside her, felt the nudge of his erection against her thigh, and anticipation rose in her once more. His mouth sought hers and she didn't need words to give her agreement. She conveyed it in her kiss, in the touch of her hands, and in her body's response.

He was going home to Greece. But before he went she would ensure she had enough memories to take her through the long, lonely nights of the future. Memories of Nick. Memories of love.

She made love to him, and morning moved into afternoon and then into evening. They stopped to eat, sharing a salad and bread and memories of Crete, then shared an evening walk, hand in hand, along the beach, before falling into bed again as evening became night.

Alex yawned after their latest lovemaking and nestled into the space between his arm and his body. With his free arm he stroked her shoulder, almost hypnotising her. It had been a perfect day. Her body felt exhausted, yet at the same time exhilarated. Muscles she'd long forgotten about already voiced their protest.

She was deliciously close to sleep. 'When are you leaving?' she asked softly.

His hand stopped and pulled away to rub his forehead. 'A few days.'

Alex felt her heart squeeze tight. She'd known he was leaving, but still disappointment consumed her. But why should one day's lovemaking make any difference to his plans? She'd never believed it would— had she?

But what of a son? Would he stay if he knew about his son?

She licked her swollen lips. 'Is there anything that might make you reconsider?'

'I have businesses back in Greece. Now that Dimitri is here, there is no reason for me to stay. I have to go.'

He didn't hesitate with his response. She should feel grateful he'd made his intentions clear. She closed her eyes and nodded into his shoulder. 'I know.'

So he was going. And tomorrow she would tell him about Jason. At least they would have a chance to meet each other before he left. Tomorrow. First thing tomorrow…

He was gone. Alex looked at the pillow next to her, devoid of everything but the impression of Nick's head. Her ears strained for sounds of running water—the shower—a kettle? But there was nothing to hear. The silence of an otherwise empty house wrapped around her. Only the sounds of early-morning bird calls drifted in from outside, like the bright needles of sunlight squeezing through the gaps in the curtains.

She reached out an arm. The bed was cold. Where was he? She sat up, looking over the edge of the bed, but the floor only held her own discarded clothes.

Suddenly wide awake, she jumped up and scrabbled into her robe, trying to ignore the ache of rarely used muscles. She checked the kitchen and bathroom. She kneeled on the sofa and looked through the front curtains. But even a peek out of the front window revealed nothing but her own car in the driveway.

She looked around the room for a note or message. But there was nothing.

Nick and every trace of him had disappeared. She collapsed down onto the sofa. Some time early in the morning he'd sneaked out of her bed and out of her life.

'You're a fool, Alex Hammond, a prize fool,' she told herself, anger replacing her shock at discovering his undercover departure. 'How could you have fallen for that?'

After all, ever since his arrival he'd been after her to jump into bed. Now she had, and where was he? Gone. Long gone.

It was clear he'd got what he wanted.

Tears pricked at her eyes, but anger at her own actions forced them back. She sniffed. 'A silly fool,' she repeated, heading off to the kitchen to put on the kettle. He'd conned her well and good. All that stuff about leaving any talk until tomorrow—well, he clearly wasn't interested. He'd had no intention of staying and hearing any of it. Clearly wasn't interested in her or her life. He never wanted to know—otherwise why wouldn't he have stuck around?

Now he would go back to Greece and never know about his son. Well, it would serve him right.

Alex jiggled a teabag while her teeth toyed with her bottom lip. Only that didn't solve anything. Nick still needed to know he had a son. But with Jason's birthday tomorrow there was no way he was going to know before the event.

She flicked the teabag out into the sink and sat down at the table, trying to get her thoughts under some sort of control.

She should have insisted on telling him about Jason before they'd made love—only it had been easier not to. She hadn't taken much convincing. There was little chance he'd have wanted to make love to her after a revelation like that, and at the time that had seemed the most important thing. Amazing how your hormones could replace logic with lust.

The phone rang and she jumped. Just maybe…

But it was Tilly, confirming what time she should arrive for the party tomorrow. Alex recited the details, trying not to sound too disappointed, and briefly explained that Sofia's 'wedding' was off. She rang off and checked the time on the wall clock, and clunked her brain out of what-ifs and back into reality.

Jason was due back after lunch. Since she'd written off yesterday she now only had a few hours to do what she needed to get done for tomorrow's holiday Monday party. She had to get moving.

CHAPTER NINE

THEY were all there. Jason and seven of his school-friends, including Matt and Jack, took turns at slapping the *piñata* hanging from the clothesline with a broomstick while Alex and Tilly escaped inside to put the final touches to the party food.

Her parents had already called from Perth, to wish Jason happy birthday and good fortune. Alex wished they could be here, but it wasn't too long until Christmas, which would be even better.

The cake was all ready—a huge chocolate mud cake, iced to resemble a soccer ball—with eight candles positioned all around, ready to be lit at the right time. She'd take that outside when they'd finished with afternoon tea.

Alex smiled to herself as she heated the last of the sausage rolls. Everything was going so well. It was a bright day, Jason was having the time of his life and the kids were all having fun. Just perfect.

The doorbell rang as she was carrying the last of the food out to the outdoor seating on the rear verandah. She hesitated, sure all the invitees were accounted for.

'I'll get it,' Tilly called. 'It's probably just someone collecting money for a good cause. You go on.'

Alex smiled gratefully and backed out through the screen door, carrying her load in both hands, to be met with squeals and yells of triumph. The final blow had been delivered to the *piñata* and sweets rained out over them. Eight boys immediately dropped to the ground, scrabbling for the most booty. She couldn't help but laugh at the sight.

She heard footsteps coming through the kitchen. 'Tilly,' she called, 'come and see. This is too funny.'

Tilly stepped through the door. 'It seems we have another guest.'

Alex turned, only to see Nick follow Tilly onto the verandah. Blood drained from her face to congeal in her gut. At just one glimpse of him memories of their lovemaking surged back, memories of being close, of how he'd pleasured her, how she'd pleasured him...

Everything had been so perfect. So why had he left? And why was he back? She tossed up her chin and looked from one to the other. 'What's going on?'

Tilly scowled at her sister. 'Hey, don't be like that. Nick just apologised for losing me the best contract I'd ever had. And he's brought Jason a present—look.'

Alex dragged her eyes down to the package he held, frowned, and then looked back to his face.

'What are you doing here?'

'I came to see you, as it happens, and I remembered what you'd said about your son's party. I hope you don't mind, only I don't have much time before I leave.'

'Of course she doesn't mind,' said Tilly. 'Lovely of him to think of Jason—don't you think, Alex?'

Alex looked at Tilly, who was smiling too encouragingly.

'I'm sure Jason will appreciate the gesture,' she went on, and Alex could swear she could just about hear Tilly's teeth grating, forcing her to respond in the affirmative.

She swallowed and forced a bare smile to her face. 'Thanks. I'm sure he'll be very pleased.'

She looked over to the boys, who were now busily comparing the spoils of war, and sought out her son. He was there, in the middle, and pain knifed through her heart. She stole a breath and found a new emotion filling the gouge the knife had made—exhilaration. After eight long years father and son would finally meet.

Would they like each other?

She called out to Jason and he looked up, noticing for the first time the stranger beside her. He stuffed the sweets into his pockets and ran over, looking curiously at the visitor.

'Jason,' she said, with one hand around his waist, as he was already getting too tall to put her arm comfortably around his shoulders any more, 'this is Mr Santos, a—colleague of mine. He wants to meet you.'

'Pleased to meet you, Jason. Happy birthday.'

He looked up at Nick, then down at the present, and then over to his mother as if checking it was okay. She smiled and nodded her head and he seemed to relax, shaking Nick's hand and saying hello.

'I forgot to get a card; I hope you don't mind,' said Nick, handing over the present.

'Nah, that's cool. Thanks, Mr Santos.'

'Call me Nick.'

Jason looked up curiously from his unwrapping. 'Sure—thanks, Nick.' Then his attention went back to the present. 'Oh, cool! Guys! Check this out. Wow! A World Cup soccer ball. Who wants to have a kick?' He turned away to share his prize with his friends and then turned back. 'Gee, thanks Mr Sa— I mean, thanks, Nick.'

Nick smiled and reached out a hand to ruffle his hair.

'My pleasure. Go and have a kick with your friends. I hear you're pretty good. I used to play a bit myself.'

Jason looked sideways up at him. 'You want a kick too?'

Nick nodded. 'Sounds good to me,' he said, heading off after Jason. Before long the small backyard was full of eight kids and Nick, standing as far apart as they could get in the tiny space, kicking the ball to each other, dribbling it around the lawn, and practising headers between them. While they practised their tackling Nick was doing some pretty fancy footwork, successfully evading the kids trying to tackle him.

Alex could do nothing but stare after them, wondering what on earth was happening. 'Close that mouth,' Tilly suggested, 'before some bird builds a nest in it.'

Alex looked at her. 'Did you see that?'

'Yep. They say boys never grow up. Looks like they're right. Now, help me get some covers for this food. I suspect afternoon tea is going to be late.'

Ten minutes later the two women sat down and watched the others play while they enjoyed a cup of coffee. Alex was glad for the chance to think. Nick had said he'd come to see her—what was that all about? Or had he remembered she wanted to talk— was that why he'd come back?

In the past day she'd tried unsuccessfully to put him out of her mind. She'd tried to come to terms with the thought she might never see him again, and yet here he was.

But in reality what chance had she had to put him out of her mind? Forty-eight hours ago they'd been in the throes of lovemaking. Just watching him made her body ache for more. Heat built up inside her and she crossed her legs, trying to suppress her growing need. It didn't seem right to think such thoughts at a child's birthday party.

Finally the players collectively decided they'd had enough. They all drifted up to the table, puffing and with sweat-spiked hair, eager for cordial and sustenance.

'Wow,' said Jason turning to Nick as he reached for a cup, 'where'd you learn to play like that?'

'Back in Greece, where I grew up.'

'You're from Greece?' He looked at his mother strangely, then focused back on Nick. *'Kalimera,'* he said. *'Kalimera*, Kyrios Santos.'

Nick stopped pouring cordial into the cups held out around him. *'Kalimera*, Jason. You speak Greek?'

'I'm learning at school. My teacher says we should practice whenever we meet someone from Greece.'

'Sounds like good advice,' he said, and resumed pouring cordial. 'Are you all learning Greek?'

A chorus of 'no' went up, with cries of 'French' and 'Spanish'.

'Why did you choose Greek, Jason?'

He shrugged as he piled up his plate with four sausage rolls, three pieces of pizza and a half-dozen cocktail frankfurters, over all of which he squeezed an unhealthy spurt of tomato sauce. 'Mum picked it. But that's okay. I like it.'

Alex was anxious to change the subject. 'Nick, I don't expect you want cordial. Can I get you something stronger—a beer or some wine, maybe?'

He looked at her, eyes narrowed. 'Thanks, but cordial is fine—really.'

She shivered as his eyes bored into her. Was he working it all out? Good for him. Whatever happened he wasn't going to be able to say she had denied her son his heritage.

'Did you two want to talk?' Tilly asked. 'I can always look after these guys for a while. They won't be getting into much mischief with their mouths full.'

'There's no need—'

'We'd appreciate it—'

Tilly looked from one to the other, smiling. 'Well, what's it to be, then?'

Alex shrugged, knowing when she was beaten and realising that the time had finally come. 'Okay,' she said, heading into the kitchen, 'follow me.'

'It will be my pleasure,' she heard him say behind her, in a way that put ripples down her spine.

It was dark inside, and it took a moment for his eyes to adjust. He'd enjoyed the determined sway of her hips as she led him into the room, and now she'd turned with her back to the kitchen sink he was enjoying the way her bust filled the soft scoop-neck T-shirt. The soft floral skirt she was wearing floated around the top of her knees, giving only a hint of the smooth legs beneath.

'Jason seems to like his present. Thank you for that.'

He shrugged. 'It was no trouble—seeing I crashed his party.' Now that his eyes had adjusted to the dim light he could see more clearly. He was about to lean against the kitchen table but thought better of it when he saw the soccer ball birthday cake sitting in pride of place. 'Nice cake,' he said, though there was something about it that jagged in his mind, something not quite right.

'I didn't expect to see you again.'

He looked up at her voice. He hadn't expected to be here. 'No, I guess not.'

'But we do have to talk…' She'd wanted to get her head around how she was going to introduce the subject of their son, but instead blurted out the first thing that came to mind. 'Why did you sneak off like that?'

Good question, he thought. *Because it was easier.* 'I thought it would be better for both of us.'

'Well, it wasn't. I had something to tell you and you didn't give me the chance.'

'I forgot.'

Truth was, he'd wanted out of there—fast. He'd known he'd enjoy the lovemaking, but that day had been something else. The sex had been incredible. Though it had gone beyond that. The day he'd spent with her had taken him back to a time he'd thought he'd never experience again. It had scared him, and his first reaction had been to run. That wasn't what he'd intended. He turned his eyes back to her and remembered what he'd been saying.

'How could I not forget—in the *heat* of the moment?'

She felt it too. He could see by her widening eyes and the way her grip tightened on the counter behind. She could feel this indefinable heat that accompanied her presence.

She cleared her throat, her hands clinging to the counter in their white knuckled grip. 'Then I'm glad you came back.'

'What is it?' he asked, curious about what was so important, and more curious about that cake, done up like a soccer ball.

Something about it didn't seem right. He looked over at it once more and it hit him.

Breath hissed in through his teeth.

'When is Jason's birthday?'

She looked taken aback for a second. She blinked and he saw her throat move as she swallowed. 'Today.'

'No,' he said, 'not his party. His birthday.'

'Today.'

Today! The anniversary of Stavros's death. What kind of coincidence was that?

'But he's seven today—correct? I thought he was seven.' Seven candles would confirm what he suspected. She'd met someone else when she'd come home and it had been his baby she'd delivered a year or so later. He indicated the cake. 'Yet I count eight candles. Did someone make a mistake?'

She looked at him and nodded, but instead of making him relieved, the look on her face made his gut clench tighter with every dip of her head.

'*I* made a mistake. I should have told you earlier.' She hesitated. 'I'm sorry, Nick. Jason is your son.'

Silence, and the seconds spun out, encompassing them both as their eyes locked true to each other.

Until finally the screen door slammed and the subject of their conversation skidded to a halt in the middle of the kitchen between them.

'Aunt Tilly says it's time for cake, before the guys have to go home.' He looked from one to the other. 'Are you guys okay? You both look kind of funny.'

Alex roused herself first. She took a deep breath and flexed her shoulders, trying to ease the building strain. 'Fine, Jason. We were just talking. I'll get the cake.'

'Okay,' he said, running once more for the door. 'Hey, guys!' he yelled before he'd cleared the door. 'Here comes the cake.' Cheers drifted in from outside.

She moved to the table, almost in slow motion, trying to keep as far away as possible from Nick as she could. *Say something,* she screamed inside. *Say anything.* But Nick didn't move a muscle until she was leaning over the cake and then he suddenly edged her aside.

'I'll do it,' he said in a voice that invited no argument. 'It's about time I was allowed to do something for my son.'

He swept the cake off the table and strode outside. Alex was left following, teeth jammed into her bottom lip. He was talking, and he was at least civil. That was something, given the circumstances. But she could see he was tightly wound up, and she just prayed he wouldn't unwind right now. She still had to tell Jason after all.

She followed him out through the door and noticed Tilly's raised eyebrows at the strange procession. Nick put the cake down on the table, to delighted oohs and aahs from the boys, and looked around.

Alex held out her hand. 'Do you want to light the candles?'

'Thank you,' he said, his words polite but his eyes cold and damning as he took the matches from her.

Tilly looked over at her, her eyes questioning. Well? she mouthed. Alex gave a brief nod and looked away, before Tilly or anyone else might see the moisture welling there.

The candles lit, Nick started the boys singing 'Happy Birthday'. Alex remembered her camera at the last minute and managed a shot of Jason blowing out each and every candle in one go. For once she didn't have to reach for the video camera. Nick was here to witness this birthday party after all.

'Now,' said Nick, after the cheers had subsided, 'make a wish.'

The boy looked at Nick, this man who all of a sudden seemed to be the one in control, a slight frown puckering his young eyebrows. Then he looked at his mother. Alex smiled and he seemed to relax a little. Then he squeezed his eyes shut for a good ten seconds.

Then he opened them and yelled, 'Bags the biggest bit.'

Nick sliced the cake into man-sized portions the boys appreciated, and before the last one had finished parents were arriving to collect their exhausted and chocolate-smeared children.

Soon only the four of them remained. Alex dreaded what was coming as she started the cleaning up. She could sense the volcano that was building inside Nick, could see the tension rising in his dark eyes, and though all remained calm on the exterior, she knew he was going to blow.

Tilly sensed it too, as they were washing up the last of the dishes in the kitchen. Nick was gazing out of the window at his son, still kicking the new soccer ball around. 'I might wander off, sis, in a little while,' she said, drying her hands on a towel. 'Do you think Jason might like to come to my place for a while?'

Nick looked up sharply. 'No!'

Tilly recoiled as if she'd been slapped. 'We'll be back, if that's what you're worried about. It just looks like you two have some unfinished business. Maybe it's better if you sort that out first, before involving my nephew.'

Nick looked at Alex. Did he really think she would try and spirit Jason away when at last they had finally met? But in his position maybe she'd be nervous about exactly the same thing. She didn't have a shiny track record in the keeping-him-informed stakes. 'They'll be back. I promise.'

He grunted something about a couple of minutes and strode outside in time to pick up a deftly aimed pass from Jason. She watched him out of the window, noticed the tension dissolving in his shoulders as his muscles freed up and they kicked the ball to each other.

And it hit her like a soccer ball into her gut. Father and son together. The picture she'd never had in her mind was now being played out in the backyard. They could be any normal family on a public holiday weekend. Father and son kicking around a football while Mum cleaned up inside. The cliché brought a sardonic smile to her face.

Tilly picked up her bag and keys. 'You be all right?'

She nodded. 'Sure. Best to get it over with. It had to happen one day, I guess.'

Tilly kissed her sister on the cheek, gave her arm a squeeze and smiled. 'I'll be back in an hour—okay? But call me on my mobile before if you need to.' She called to Jason and he came running, soccer ball in his arms. After a quick peck on his cheek, they were gone.

Alex waved from the front door and knew the moment he stepped up behind her—knew by the prickle of her skin, by the scent of man—hot, angry man. Every nerve cell screamed his presence. Except this time it was for all the wrong reasons.

This time she felt afraid.

'Thank you for inviting me to my son's eighth birthday,' he said from behind her.

She closed her eyes, made a mental prayer for strength, and turned to face him.

'I would have, if you hadn't bolted from my bed without a word.'

He glared at her. 'You say that now. How am I supposed to believe you? You have lied to me for eight years—even longer! Why should you start telling the truth now?'

'I never lied to you!'

'So what do you call more than eight years of silence? Eight years of hiding my son from me. Eight years of depriving me of seeing my son grow up. What is that if not a lie?'

'I didn't lie—'

'And when would you have told me if I hadn't turned up in Sydney? If I hadn't turned up on your doorstep today? How much longer would you have made me wait for the truth? I would never have found out about Jason being my son. You would never have told me.'

He took a few steps around the room, picking up a photograph at random and moving on to the next.

'I've already missed out on eight years of his life. How much more would you have had me miss?'

Suddenly she moved to an old chest of drawers in the corner of the room. She pulled out the bottom drawer. 'Look,' she said, holding one of the stash of folders contained within. 'I have photos—lots of photos—and...' She pulled out the next drawer. 'Videos. Every birthday. Jason when he was newborn, in the bath, his first steps. I have them all on video...'

'You have had my son for eight years and all you offer me is videos?'

She dropped the folder back in the drawer and pushed it shut, realising how pathetic her offer sounded. He was right. She'd been a fool all these years, thinking that somehow a picture every now and then or a few minutes of film was going to somehow make up for years of absence.

'And where is his father in these videos? You have deprived my son of a father for eight years. How could you be so selfish?'

Selfish! After eight years of struggling by herself to create some sort of security for her child—years when her own youth had been put aside so she could be a young mother to a child no one had asked for but was there to be cared for and loved nonetheless—to hear that word used about her stung deep. She swallowed down the burn at the back of her throat, fought the prick of tears that was threatening. She sniffed.

'He's my son too, don't forget.'

'How could I forget? He must be your son. Not once did you intimate that I might be involved.' He paused for a second, revelation bright in his eyes. 'That's why you resigned, isn't it? So you wouldn't have to tell me. So I would never find out.'

She gulped, shook her head. 'It wasn't like that... I can explain...'

In three strides he had crossed the room between them and stood before her, gripping her arms and glaring down at her so that she felt small and powerless.

'Then what was it like? Why did you never tell me? Why did you let me believe he was another man's child? Why did you never tell me when he was born?'

'I didn't think you'd believe me.'

'What?'

'We used a condom. He shouldn't have happened. Why would you believe me?'

'But a baby. How could you keep that secret from his father?'

She swallowed back a sob. 'I know. I rang the day he was born—remember. I rang to tell you. But it was the day—'

'The day Stavros died,' he finished, dropping her arms and wheeling around. 'We could have done with some good news that day.'

She laughed—a harsh, brittle laugh that sounded as if at any moment it would fracture in the tense, heated air between them.

She rubbed her arms where they still stung, as if he had branded her. 'It wouldn't have been good news—not to your family.'

'Not good news? My family lurched from one nightmare to the next after that. Don't you think we deserved a bit of happiness? Something to look forward to—a child for me—a grandchild for my parents?'

'An *illegitimate* grandchild for your parents. The second—remember?'

He brushed her words away with a firm sweep of his arm.

'That child was never Stavros's!'

'But Stavros believed he was. He went against your parents' wishes. He married the mother, believing he was doing the right thing.'

'She wanted his money—'

'Yes, and so did her boyfriend. He wanted the family to pay up—hush money. But the plan went wrong and Stavros acted from the heart. So she won a bigger prize—she married into the Santos family and drove her boyfriend crazy with jealousy until he couldn't stand that she wasn't coming back and killed Stavros.'

'What has this to do with you not telling me?'

She looked at him, momentarily dumbstruck.

'Don't you remember how you felt all the months leading up to Stavros's death? Month after month you would tell me how the situation had worsened. How your parents would not accept the girl. How she flouted Stavros's will and spent his money as fast as she could, leaving the baby in the care of full-time nanny.'

She took a deep breath.

'Then you told me how Stavros had realised what a mistake he had made. When I found out I was pregnant they had only just been married. I thought it was so romantic of him to defy his parents and marry for love. But I knew how much his family, including you, were against the marriage. And there was me, wanting so much for their marriage to work out.'

She stopped talking but he remained silent, totally unresponsive to her story. What impact her words had had she couldn't tell. His jawline remained firm and set and his eyes glinted with anger still. She ran her tongue over dry lips.

'But things didn't improve. They got worse. And

as they grew worse I grew more and more afraid to tell you. I knew your parents would never believe me. I knew you would never believe me.'

'How can you say that?'

'Because you never believed her story either. Stavros had used protection, you told me. You thought she was lying. Why, then, should you believe me?'

'She was lying!'

Her chin lifted a tad. 'Absolutely. So you weren't about to fall for that old trick again.'

She could see his jaw working as his teeth ground together.

'I still had a right to know!' he said at last.

She nodded in agreement, and when she spoke her voice was more resigned. She picked up one of the photos sitting on the mantel nearby. Jason had only been two days old, wrapped in his blue hospital shawl, his alert dark eyes absorbing everything. She smiled.

'I know. That's why I rang the day Jason was born. I looked into his beautiful face and knew you had to be told. So I rang—' Her voice cracked as she remembered that day, the stresses, the excitement and afterglow of birth, and the anticipation of speaking to Nick and sharing their wonderful news. Only to hear of the family's shocking tragedy first.

When she looked up his eyes were shiny, blurred behind tears of pain, and she knew he was remembering too.

'Do you think your family—you included—would have been interested in my news?' She hesitated. 'You had suddenly become the heir. When you were the younger brother I had thought it possible—maybe, if Stavros could make it work—that you and me—and Jason—might make a go of it together. But when Stavros died I couldn't do it to you—not after that.'

'So it seems Stavros and I have something in common. We both fell for women who were born liars.'

She shook her head.

'She lied to trap Stavros. I never tried to trap you. I did everything I could to protect you.'

He spun on his heel and looked to the ceiling, his hands clasped behind his head and his chest heaving in air. It seemed like for ever before he turned, and by then the sheen in his eyes had gone and pure steel blazed out from them.

'But eight years! In eight years you haven't tried to set that to rights. You have made no attempt to call or send news or even any of this vast photograph collection you claim to have been keeping for me. You have kept my child from me.'

She looked away, hanging her head. 'I guess that's how it looks.' Then she looked up. 'But that wasn't my intention, Nick. Never my intention. You have to believe me.'

'No. I don't think I should believe anything you say. It seems you have hidden this secret for eight years. What else are you hiding?'

'I don't know what you mean.'

'Is there more you should tell me that you haven't? Has the boy suffered any serious medical conditions? Is he having trouble at school?'

'What? You've seen for yourself he's perfectly well. And his grades are in the top ten per cent for his age. I have a folder with his school results. Do you want to see those?'

He waved her offer aside with a flick of his wrist. 'Don't be so outraged. I can't trust you to tell me the truth. It's no wonder I have to ask directly. Expect many more questions as I come to learn about my son.'

'*Our* son.'

His lips curled into a sardonic smile as he took a couple of steps towards her. 'Oh? So now he's "our" son? How very generous of you.'

She shrugged off his sarcasm. He had a right to feel aggrieved, after all. Though that was no reason to forget Jason was still her son too. 'I know you have some catching up to do. We'll have to make some arrangements. You can visit any time you like. I'm sure Jason would like that.'

He raised an eyebrow. 'I'm sure he would. But I think after all this time we both deserve more.'

A cold sliver of fear wedged its way down her spine. 'What do you mean?'

'Simple. You've had my son for eight years. Now it's my turn. I'm taking him home to Greece.'

CHAPTER TEN

'No! You can't do that!'

Pure dread clutched at her heart.

'Why not? I see a certain symmetry in the plan—a certain equity, wouldn't you say? Eight years with you—eight years with me. You can come and collect him on his sixteenth birthday—if he still remembers you.'

'You can't mean that!'

His lip curled at the edge and he shook his head fractionally. 'You really believe I have become such a monster? Well, maybe I have.'

He turned his head away, so he wouldn't be distracted by the panic in her eyes, the ice-blue terror he could see welling there. But there was no other way. She'd given him no choice—not after what she'd done.

He would make it as easy as possible for the boy—Dimitri would have contacts. He'd arrange the best care, the best school. He'd find the top soccer coaches. His son would have the best of everything.

And he would have his son.

He turned back, his mind made up.

'The boy will come with me.'

'All the way to Greece? How can you do that to

him? Don't you realise what a shock that will be for him?'

'But, my dear Alexandra, don't you appreciate what a good job you've done in preparing him for this? He plays soccer, our national sport, and he's already speaking Greek. He will be right at home.'

'But this is his home!'

He looked around, as if assessing and finding it lacking. 'I can give him more. I can give him his birthright. He doesn't need to live like this.'

Fingernails biting into her palms, Alex struggled to remember to breathe.

'Like *what*, exactly?'

He shrugged. 'All these years you've been doing it tough, getting by with what you have. Jason deserves better—he could have so much more—he *should* have so much more. I can give it to him.'

'That's not fair. There's more to life than money.'

'Don't talk to me about fair! You kept my child secret for eight years. Denied me what is rightfully mine. You're the *least* qualified person to decide what is and what isn't fair. My son is coming to Greece. It's settled. I'll make the arrangements.'

'You can't just do that. He can't go. He doesn't even have a passport.'

That took him by surprise, she could see. He wouldn't have imagined for a minute that Jason wouldn't have a passport.

'How long will it take to get one?'

'One week, maybe two—*if* I agree to sign the papers.'

He moved up next to her and held the back of her head with his hand, so that she couldn't look anywhere but into his deep, dark eyes. Her hands pressed against his chest. She could feel the hard nub of his nipples with her fingers as she tried to stop her body colliding full length with his.

She could feel his heartbeat, slow and strong under her fingers, and knew that her own was beating crazily at least at twice the rate. For a second she thought he was going to kiss her, and confusion muddied her thoughts. Her lips parted, though whether it was from anticipation or the shock of his sudden proximity she couldn't be sure.

But instead of his mouth he brushed one finger over her lips, and breath infused with the scent of him stuck in her throat.

'Oh, you'll sign. You've got a lot to make up for.'

From outside came the sound of a car pulling into the driveway. Nick's eyes were drawn to the window, but Alex didn't need to look to realise Tilly and Jason were back already.

'Ah, my son is back,' announced Nick, letting her go and moving away. 'I take it you haven't told Jason anything?'

Still too disturbed by his touch, she confirmed it with a nod of her head.

'Then it's time we did.'

Alex raced after him as he headed for the door.

Five minutes later Tilly had departed and Jason had been settled on the sofa with a glass of milk, his free hand patting the soccer ball alongside.

'We've got something to tell you, Jason,' Alex started, kneeling on the carpet near where he sat, her hands tightly clasped together to resist the temptation to reach out and flick the blade of grass welded to his knee. If she touched him now she'd be too tempted to pull him into her arms and protect him for ever from secrets and their consequences. But one sidelong look at Nick and it was clear nothing would protect either of them.

He shifted alongside, showing his impatience at her hesitation. She pressed her lips together, concentrating on the words to come. 'Only it might come as a bit of a shock.'

Jason looked at them both in turn, his serious expression completely at odds with the milky-white smile left by his drink. Without saying a word he leaned forward, settled the glass on the coffee table in front of him, and sat back, his breath coming out in a huff. 'Is this anything to do with Mr Sant— I mean, Nick being my dad?'

Alex reeled back, but still caught the shock flash across Nick's face. 'Yes…but how did you know?'

'I made a wish when I blew my candles— Er, am I allowed to tell you that, now that it's come true?' he asked sheepishly.

She mussed his hair. 'Of course.'

'Is he the man in those letters?'

'Ah.' She licked her lips and looked to the floor.

Nick frowned. 'What letters?'

'Mum's got a box of letters in the cupboard from someone called Nick. She said he was her boyfriend before I was born. That was you—wasn't it?'

He looked at Jason and nodded. 'That was me.' Then he looked at Alex, who shook her head.

'I was…cleaning up. Had forgotten they were there.'

His face impassive, he looked back to his son and smiled. 'So, Jason, how would you like to come and visit Greece with me—get some real practice with your Greek language skills?'

'Greece? You mean it? That would be so cool. Wait till I tell the guys at school.'

'Only if you're sure, Jason. It's a long way to go, and you might stay there for a while. You might want to wait till end of term?'

'No way. How soon do we go?'

Alex tried to smile, but it was so hard, with her heart tearing its way through the floor, leaving jagged edges and bleeding veins in its wake.

Suddenly he threw himself forward, winding his arms around his mother's neck. 'Thanks, Mum. This is the best birthday ever. Can I take my soccer ball?'

She sniffed and hung on tight, and tried to ignore the threatening stab of tears. 'I'm sure you can,' was all she could manage.

'Cool.' As quickly as he had jumped on her he

released her and picked up the ball. 'Can I go play out in the back now?'

Alex nodded—it was easier than speaking with this huge sense of loss hovering at the back of her throat.

As much as she hated the idea of him leaving her, there was no way she could deny him a passport and the chance to see his other home. It was only fair that he knew both.

She would lose him as quickly as he had run out through that door. In a week or two, or however long it took, Jason would leave for the other side of the world and Alex would be left with nothing.

'I hope you're satisfied,' she said at last, wiping the tears from her eyes with the back of her hand.

Nick grunted and slapped his legs with his hands. 'So—tomorrow I want you to make arrangements for a passport. I'll arrange the tickets.'

She sniffed. 'And then you will take my son away from me.'

'Like you took him from me.' His words came as a harsh grating sound.

'No. It's not the same thing. You didn't know he existed until now. I have loved this child for more than eight years—nurtured him, held him when he was sick and cheered with him when he achieved every new goal.' Her voice was a bare whisper but she had to continue. She had to make him realise what he was costing her. 'For you to take him from me now, after all that, it's much, much worse.'

Her voice threatening to break, she had to stop.

Had to get out of the space Nick was consuming and into the kitchen. He had come into her house and consumed her and her life like a vacuum. He had sucked her life dry.

A month ago she'd had a job, a new home and a son she loved more than anything. Nick had turned all of that upside down. Now she had to find another job, some way of meeting her home-loan repayments. Now she'd lost her self-respect after a day of love-making that had left her with nothing but bittersweet memories. And now she was going to lose Jason, the brightest light in her life and the person who gave her a reason to go on. Nick was taking him away.

To think that two days ago she'd finally admitted she still loved Nick. What good had that realisation done her?

Nick had always been going to go back to Greece, and she had looked forward to the day with a mixture of anticipation and sorrow. His departure would have been bad enough to bear—to lose him for the second time. But now that pain would be surpassed by a greater, more devastating agony. Now he was taking their son with him.

Now she would lose them both.

Nick spent every chance he could in the following days to be with Jason and get to know him better. He even chose to play babysitter when Alex had her night classes. It was hard to begrudge him his presence as it was clear he was genuinely interested in their son.

On the weekend Nick decided on an outing—a 'family outing', he'd said—and chose the zoo. Jason responded with his usual zeal for everything about Nick. Nick could do no wrong in Jason's eyes, ever since he'd appeared bearing his soccer ball gift.

'Beware of Greeks bearing gifts.' The old proverb ran through her mind. How appropriate, she reflected, just a bit too late.

But part of her knew this was right. It was the way things should be between a father and a son, and Nick was taking to the role of father as if he'd been born to it. As for Jason, he was revelling in it. It was as if all his dreams had come true.

Alex suppressed a sigh. For her the nightmare was about to begin. In a few days Jason's passport would be ready and he would leave. She had no idea how she was going to survive after that. She could have avoided coming today, but she didn't want to miss a chance of being with Jason before he left.

She looked around, scanning the crowd for Nick, who'd gone to buy ice creams while Jason was entertained by the antics of a wild-haired orang-utan, climbing up and then jumping off his pole. Again and again he did the same routine, clapping when he reached the top of the pole, encouraging his audience to applaud likewise.

Jason gripped her hand tightly, pointing at the animal and laughing madly.

Without notice the orang-utan suddenly changed his routine. He jumped down from the pole, but instead of climbing right back up he made a dash towards his audience, took a flying leap, and crashed into the perimeter fence right in front of them. The entire crowd gasped and instantly recoiled, before spontaneously breaking out into laughter. Jason was no exception—he had all but leaped into his mother's arms—and shook with laughter as the orang-utan bobbed up and down in front of them, obviously feeling very self-satisfied.

Nick stood holding the ice creams just to one side, watching Alex hold Jason. She was laughing out loud, laughing so hard she had to wipe the tears from her eyes.

It was good to see her laugh. She hadn't been doing much of it lately. Her face looked drawn and her eyes were shadowed and dull. But for now she was laughing, her face bright and beautiful, her hands on Jason's shoulders as his own laughter subsided.

And something shifted inside Nick—something vague and harsh-edged tilted and swung, lodging into a place deep inside and grating with every intake of breath so that he felt himself frown.

He still wanted her, and after last week's lovemaking he wanted her more than ever. That surprised him. But what was more surprising was that he wasn't angry with her any more. Last week's cold fury had been replaced by something else—something that felt more like regret, that things hadn't worked out differently all those years ago.

Alex turned, the smile still on her face where it

froze, only her eyes showing surprise that he was watching them. He shook off the frown and the mess of unusual emotions crashing through him and smiled back, holding up the ice creams triumphantly. Finally her smile edged up near her eyes and she moved Jason's shoulders around so he could see what was coming.

'Ice cream!' he yelled. 'Cool!'

They wandered around the zoo, eating their ice creams and watching the animals. And when they'd finished their ice creams they walked hand in hand, Jason between them, around the park. They shared a picnic under shady trees with all the other families, and then Jason showed Nick how to feed the kangaroos and Alex took photos of the two of them until a man took the camera and snapped the three of them together. Then they walked some more, and somehow Nick ended up between Jason and Alex, holding hands as they strolled around.

It was nine-thirty before they were home and Jason had finally gone to bed, and Nick suggested a glass of wine to finish the evening.

She nodded. 'Please,' she replied, feeling tired and dreamy. Usually she couldn't wait for Nick to leave, but today had been such a wonderful day—a day when they'd come the closest ever to being a family. It couldn't last—she knew that—and because of that she was reluctant to let it end.

In the still warm air they sat on the verandah, moths dancing around the soft outside light to the accompaniment of the noises of a suburb settling down to sleep, and the distant whoosh of the slip of waves across the shore.

He set the wine glasses down on the table between them and sat down alongside. Neither spoke for a long time.

She was weary, but comfortable, and for once felt relaxed in Nick's presence. It was as if she had worked out her tension in the exertions and laughter of Taronga Zoo, and now she was content to just be there. Whatever happened, whatever her future, she would treasure today's memories for a long time.

And she could honestly say that she was happy with the way things were working out between Nick and Jason. She could never have let Jason go to Greece if he hadn't liked his newfound father, or if Nick hadn't treated him well. But things were working out better than anyone could possibly have predicted. Despite all the cynicism Nick had shown towards family life, he'd taken to his new role admirably. It was clear the two had built a solid foundation on which to develop their relationship further in Greece. That at least was some consolation. For some time soon she'd have to tell Jason that he was going to Greece without her. The better he got to know Nick before then, the more comfortable he'd feel with the whole arrangement.

She sighed and reached for her glass.

'Tired?' he asked, his voice soft and husky, as if he was trying not to interrupt the evening quiet.

She looked over at him and nodded, surprised he was so in tune with her mood. With the light behind him, his face was in shadow. It should have had the effect of making him more dangerous, but tonight it softened his features, so that they blended in the dim light, and instead of feeling threatened by him she felt warm and comfortable and relaxed.

Maybe it was the wine. The wine combined with a long, exhausting day. Maybe she'd had enough. She put her glass back down, letting her arm rest over the arm of the chair for a second. His hand closed over hers, coaxing her fingers away from the stem of the glass so that his hand completely surrounded hers.

She wasn't surprised. They'd held hands today, just like friends. It was nice, that was all.

His hand was warm. Warm and comfortable, just like he looked, and his thumb gently stroked the back of her hand, matching the rhythm of the waves so that it was almost as if it was the foam from the waves caressing her skin. She closed her eyes and let the sensation wash through her. His gentle massage was as intoxicating as the wine—gentle, slightly sweet, and with an afterglow that warmed her to the core.

He changed grip and let his fingers dance across her palm, tickling and sending waves of tingling sensation up her arm. His hand stroked the skin of her wrist, tracing a line up to her elbow and heating the blood in her veins lying underneath. She breathed deeply, feeling the flesh of her breasts firm and peak, realising that something was changing. This was suddenly much more than holding hands.

She opened her eyes to see him staring at her. He'd changed too. Now he didn't look warm and comfortable any more. Even with his face in shadow his eyes sparked with desire, and the look he sent her was laden with white heat. Breath caught in her throat as her own desires kicked up a notch in response.

He wanted her. It was in his eyes and in his touch. And if he kept looking at her that way, touching her that way, then he'd know she wanted him too.

And she didn't want him to know that. Didn't want him to know that even when he was taking her son away from her she was still not immune to his body. It was bad enough facing up to it herself. The last thing she wanted was for him to know it too.

His face dipped to her hand and his mouth brushed her skin, a warm dance of lips and heated breath before settling into a kiss that suggested so much more. She gasped, her heart skipping a beat, as his tongue grazed her skin and promised more heat, more moisture, more contact.

Desire and panic welled up inside her in equal measure. She sat up, tugging her arm from his, and rose unsteadily to her feet.

'I think it's time you left.'

He looked up at her, his eyes telling her he didn't believe a word. Her own pleaded back.

'Please,' she stressed.

Then he nodded and rose, smoothing the denim of his jeans. 'As you wish.'

Her eyes followed the movement and she almost wished they hadn't. The swell of his jeans both inflamed her and told her she'd been right to stop. There was only one place they'd been heading. She'd been there before. For a few brief moments there would be paradise, a world of passion and heightened sensations beyond belief, but afterwards would come regret, the bitter taste of hollow lovemaking, of wasted emotion and empty tomorrows.

So why did she still want him? Shouldn't it be easier than this, knowing she was right?

He took her hand and she looked up at him, surprised. 'Come on,' he said, 'you can still see me to the door.'

She nodded, not trusting herself to speak with the mess of emotions swirling inside, and obediently followed him inside.

He paused outside Jason's room. The door was ajar and a slant of moonlight cut across his bed, glowing across his sleeping face, his lips slightly parted. One arm tucked his teddy in close, the other was flung back, as if reaching for Nick's soccer ball, resting nearby.

They stood shoulder to shoulder in the doorway, watching him sleep, watching his steady breaths and angelic child's face.

And when she looked up at Nick he was staring

down at her with so much unspoken in his eyes that it passed, tremor-like, through her.

'He is a beautiful boy,' he whispered. 'Beautiful, like his mother. And strong. You have done a good job looking after him.'

She swallowed as his eyes continued to hold hers. She wanted to say that she hadn't just been looking after him, that bringing up Jason had been her life, her mission, but she didn't want to argue the point. The day had been far too special to spoil it by bickering.

And she had more to think about besides, as his fingers left hers and smoothed across her jeans, gently but insistently pulling her around and closer, so that she soon pressed up against him, so close that she could feel him harden against her belly. Even as her shoulders reared back his mouth came down and claimed hers.

She had expected his kiss to be hard and strong, expected him to try to subdue her with his sudden attack. But as his lips met hers there was no ferocity, no ambush. Instead his mouth gentled, his lips caressed hers, coaxing them to open, inviting her to join with him. The passion was there. She could feel it under the surface. But he was waiting for her.

Somehow that was the most wonderful thing. Maybe he'd stopped thinking of her as an easy target. Maybe he felt something for her after all, even if it was only as the mother of his son. Maybe he didn't just want to take her at his child's door.

Whatever, he was waiting for her to decide, and his generous gesture squeezed her heart, forcing two tears from her eyes.

It wasn't that she didn't want to make love to him. But hadn't he taken enough? Why did he want more? There was no more she could give without losing herself entirely.

Finally, as if sensing her lack of response, he pulled back and sucked in a deep breath, looking down at her, his eyes warm and enquiring. His fingers brushed her face, wiping away the tears. He frowned, and to avoid the questions in his eyes she glanced at Jason.

'You should go,' she whispered, breathless and dizzy and hoping he would take her advice, and knowing that if he argued the point she would be lost.

He chose not to argue, but let her go and led her to the front door, where he stopped for a moment before turning back. 'I want you to know Jason will be in excellent hands back in Greece. Dimitri has recommended someone excellent to look after the boy.'

Her back stiffened and she crossed her arms. 'What do you mean?'

'Just that I've been away a long time. I have a business to take care of. Obviously I won't be able to spend as much time with him as I would like—at least for a while.'

The comfortable and warm feelings he'd been stirring in her all evening began to slide off. Visions of Jason, alone and abandoned or, even worse, with a stranger in some huge empty mausoleum of a house plagued her mind. That wasn't the picture Nick had been selling to them both. How could he do that to their son?

'Maybe you should have thought about that before you decided to steal him away from me.'

It was clear from his eyes what he thought of that, and his words confirmed it. 'It is hardly stealing to take what is already mine.'

'But why do it if you know you can't look after him? Why rip him away from his home, his school, his friends, from *me*, when you know you don't have the time to commit to him? Do you really think it's fair to do all that to an eight-year-old boy?'

'He will have a new school, make new friends, and, as I said, he will have the best carer.'

'If you have to do that, why not let me come and I'll look after him?'

The thought had sprung from nowhere, but she would do anything to prevent Jason being left alone and afraid in a foreign country. She had no doubt that Nick would treat him well when he was there. They both got on so well with each other. But Nick's cool announcement that he would not have time to devote to Jason terrified her.

Who was this stranger he was about to entrust their child to? He had no idea himself.

'No.' Nick's abrupt denial cut through her like a frozen knife. 'That is not an option.'

'What do you mean—it's ''not an option''? You need someone to look after Jason. He'll be happy with me there. And I'm available.' Couldn't he see how perfect it was? She didn't have to lose Jason. Nick could have him, but she didn't have to lose him. She choked back an ironic laugh. 'Let's face it, I've no job any more. No way of paying for this house. And when you take Jason I'll have nothing left. It's a perfect option.'

He shook his head. 'No.'

'But why?'

He stared, his face angled against the harsh streetlight so that the hard planes, the cold eyes, were back. 'You need to ask?'

'So you're punishing me? This is my payback for bringing up Jason by myself? For struggling to give him a home?'

'Drop the martyr act, Alexandra, it doesn't suit you. If you like it's your payback for keeping my son a secret. For denying me my son for eight years.'

'Come on! Do you really believe you would have welcomed him back then?'

'I guess we'll never know—seeing you never bothered to give me the opportunity.' He pulled his car keys from his pocket. 'I want to know as soon as that passport arrives.'

With that he turned and pointed the remote at his car, unlocking the doors. Then he was gone, in a cloud of rich petrol fumes and burning rubber.

Alex stood at the door for a while, her soul bruised and bloodied and her blood boiling after their latest run-in. So much for not wanting to bicker and risk spoiling the day. The day and the mood it had engendered in her had been completely and utterly ruined.

Would he never forgive her? Today at times he had felt like a friend, a very good friend, and not long ago she could have led him to her bed if she had so wished.

Clearly he was still attracted to her—enough to share a bed while he was here at least. It was disappointing that her earlier impressions of him were so spot-on.

He wanted her body. He wanted their son. But there was nothing beyond that. He didn't want her.

He drove along the coast a long way, not caring where he was going, just wanting the wind to blow away the anxiety churning through his mind and the heat pooling in his groin.

Not that the combination was so much of a novelty. Both conditions seemed to go hand in hand with his dealings with Alexandra.

He hadn't realised how angry he still was. For a while lust had overridden that. Spending all day alongside her had almost been too much to bear. And she would have made love tonight if he had pressed, he was sure—what had stopped her?

Even after their final heated words, he still burned for her. Wanting her was like an ache that never went. Even those years they were apart—the pain had been duller, but it had still been there, brought into sharp and stark relief the minute she'd walked into the office that morning. If he'd thought last week's day of lovemaking would take away the burning need for her, he had been wrong. The pain was there, like a needle, only growing sharper with every fix.

Her refusal this evening had honed the edge, and even her fiery words as they'd parted couldn't dull the ache. He wanted her, whatever she had done. To deny it was to deny his very existence. But did that mean he had to forgive her?

He'd already missed out on eight years of his son's life. How much more would he have missed if not for his uncle's strange bequest?

And all because she'd lied to him. She'd kept their son a secret—a secret he might not know about now if he hadn't arrived so unexpectedly.

Why was it that lies and secrets featured so strongly in the Santos family line? First his brother and now him. Stavros's wife's lies had cost him his life. Stavros had believed her, had fallen for her lies and paid the ultimate price.

Nick's hands tightened on the steering wheel. His brother had been crazy for the woman, refusing to listen to anyone, to believe anything other than her sordid lies. He'd had to be crazy to accept her claims he was the father. He had been so blind with lust and love he hadn't even insisted on DNA testing, as everyone had advised.

She was a lying, scheming witch and he would make sure she rotted in prison along with her jealous lover. It was the only thing he could do for his brother now.

They were all the same. Stavros's wife and Alexandra—women who lied their way to what they wanted. Women who made you burn with need and took what they wanted.

She was right. It was payback time. Women like her deserved to be paid back for the lies they had told, for the truths not disclosed, for the harm they had done.

She deserved it.

He knew that, recognised it as truth, and still it didn't ease the congestion in his mind. Still something didn't make sense.

Because one woman had lied to marry into his family, while the other had done all she could to stay right away. One woman had schemed to win money and influence and power, while the other had spent her life scraping by, living on the margin as a single mother. Why would she do that when Nick could have provided for them both?

He changed down a gear and manoeuvred the sports car to a halt, suddenly annoyed with the direction both his car and his thoughts were now taking.

It was late. The moon slanted low in the sky and the stars winked down at him knowingly. He looked at them—the answer was out there, somewhere. Just like those stars that looked as if he could reach out a hand and take his pick—the answer was there, almost within his grasp but not quite.

He dropped his head and rolled his neck, trying to ease the tension in his shoulders. The drive was supposed to relax him, help him unwind, but it wasn't working. He turned the key in the ignition, heard the powerful purr of the engine and threw the car into first.

Soon he'd be home, back in Greece and with his son. He was wasting his time even thinking about anything else.

Alex was kneeling on the floor, attempting to pack the remaining piles of gear in Jason's bedroom. It wasn't all going to fit. She'd have to rearrange it or leave some things behind.

The passport had arrived early in the week. She'd lifted the unmistakable envelope from the mailbox and felt the bands around her heart tighten. The last barrier to Jason leaving was gone. The last barrier to Nick leaving was gone.

They would both be gone the day after tomorrow.

It was impossible not to think about it. Not to wonder how her life could go on without Jason's presence, not to wonder how she could go on alone.

She had three months until her first visit. Nick had at least conceded she could do that, but it was going to be the longest three months of her life.

She heard a car pull up in front. 'He's here!' yelled Jason. But Alex didn't need to be told. She knew it was him, could feel his presence in the prickle of the hairs of her neck and the sudden alertness of every cell in her body.

The front door opened and she heard Jason greeting his father in their now familiar Greek, crashing into his arms. She was going to miss her boy and the way he did everything at top speed and at full volume. Life was about to get one whole lot quieter, that was for sure.

And then they were there, at the doorway. Nick was casually dressed in black jeans and an open-necked white shirt that only accentuated his olive skin and dark features. She swallowed, as always affected by the impact of his sheer presence, and tucked a strand of hair back behind her ears.

'Hi,' she managed.

He swung a brand-new suitcase into the room. 'I wondered if you needed this? Jason seems to have a lot of gear.'

'He does,' she responded. 'I'm a bit overwhelmed by how much there is. Thanks.'

'And she hasn't even started packing her own stuff yet, have you, Mum?'

Nick frowned and flashed her a questioning look. She shook her head at Nick and flashed Jason a smile. 'Don't worry. What time is Matt's dad picking you up for your playover?'

'He's late already.' He cocked an ear as a car horn tooted. 'Oh, hang on.' He disappeared down the hallway and was back in a second. 'Gotta go—see you later, guys.'

He dashed for the front door, with Alex following him out to talk to Matt's father about what time they'd be back. And then they were gone and Alex turned back into the house.

Nick was waiting for her, angled against the doorframe with his hands and legs crossed. He didn't look happy.

'Thanks for the suitcase,' she offered, trying to work out how she was going to get by without touching him. 'I was wondering how I was going to fit everything in.'

'Avoiding the truth again?'

'What do you mean?'

'When were you thinking of telling him?'

Alex's mind hit onto his wavelength. 'Oh, I thought I would tomorrow.'

'You're sure about that? You weren't planning on telling him you wouldn't be coming just before he was about to get on the plane with me?'

'Now what are you talking about?'

'Maybe you were hoping to create a scene at the airport—*Boy ripped from mother's loving arms by foreign father*? Is that what you had in mind? The local press would love that.'

'Forget it, Nick. If I'd wanted to stop you leaving then I never would have signed his passport application.'

'Unless you want me to be embarrassed.'

'You're crazy,' she said, and pushed past him, not even trying to avoid touching him she was so angry.

He lashed out and grabbed her arm. 'Am I? You seem to have a singular ability to avoid telling the truth until it slaps you in the face. Why wouldn't you tell him, unless you were planning to embarrass me? Why leave it so late? Unless avoiding the truth really has become habit-forming for you?'

Using all the fury she felt, she yanked her arm out of his grip.

'Why wouldn't I tell him? He's my son—'

'And mine!'

'Yes! But he's a child, not a possession. And I know him. Yes, I could have told him a week ago— but why would I tell him he's being sent to Greece with a father he's never known and all by himself? Why do that to him before he's had a chance to get to know that person?'

'We get on fine.'

'I know. I think you have the makings of an excellent relationship. But any relationship takes time to develop and that's why I waited. Even when I tell him it's probably going to come as a shock that I won't be on that plane. He's spent the last eight years of his life with me and he's known you for—what? Ten days? Yes, he's going on a wonderful adventure with someone he's grown to like. But he's going to feel less secure than if I'm with him.'

'When is he returning?'

She looked up cautiously, feeling her eyes narrow. 'Why?'

'Because you are incapable of telling the truth. I will tell him myself.'

'Oh, and which version of the truth will you tell him?'

'The only one. There is only one truth here, and that is that he is coming to Greece with me—alone.'

'And will you tell him that he is going to be looked after by a nanny, a stranger, because you will be too busy to spend time with him? Will you tell him that when I suggested I should come along you refused me? And if—no, in fact *when* he wants me to come, can you imagine how learning that will make him feel? Will you tell him everything, or just the part you want him to know?'

Something harsh like a snarl erupted from deep inside him, and he closed the space between them and grabbed her arms.

'Now suddenly I'm to believe you're the expert on what constitutes truth?'

'No. I never claimed to be an expert. I'm simply saying that sometimes the truth is not so easy to define. Sometimes there's more than one truth. Sometimes there's a different take on truth.'

'I know what you're saying, but you don't get out of keeping my son a secret that easily. Your version of the truth is no better than a lie.'

'I never lied to you. I didn't think your family was ready to hear the truth back then. Maybe it was a bad call, and it made revealing the truth later on that much harder, but it was my call.'

'Just like that woman claiming Stavros was her child's father. That was her call. That was a bad call too.'

She looked at him, saw the anger and pain mixed in his eyes and realised just how much his family's tragedies had affected him. He wielded the scars like shields.

'I didn't kill Stavros, Nick. When are you going to stop blaming me? When are you going to stop punishing me for it?'

CHAPTER ELEVEN

HE LET her go as quickly as he had grabbed hold of her, wheeling away. 'That doesn't make sense.'

'Doesn't it?' She shook her head and rubbed her arms where he had branded her. 'I'm on your side, Nick. What that woman did to Stavros was beyond belief. She lied to Stavros for one reason—she wanted your family's money.'

'But you said you wanted their marriage to succeed.'

'Of course I wanted that—in the beginning. I was pregnant myself by that stage. I thought that if Stavros, the heir, could have a successful marriage on such a foundation as an unexpected baby, then there was hope for our relationship—for you and me and for our baby. I had no idea she was lying. And I saw what her betrayal did to your family. I saw it in your letters. I felt it in your words.

'The worse things got with Stavros, the harder it was for me to tell you. You hated her. Hated her for tricking him into marriage. Hated her for cheating her way into the family on the basis of a suspect pregnancy.

'You talk of speaking the truth. Of course I wanted to share the news of my pregnancy with you—but

157

would you yourself have been prepared to announce another unexpected pregnancy in such an atmosphere? In a family already divided and pained with mistrust, savage emotion and ultimately tragedy? I doubt it. The Nick I knew then would have wanted to save his family any more pain.'

She stopped, as much to allow her to catch her breath as to see if her words were getting through, and she realised she'd made herself sound far too noble.

'Besides, I was a coward.' He looked up sharply, but she bade him to remain silent while she finished. 'I was scared of your family's reaction. Scared they'd hate me for what had happened. Scared they'd brand me a liar and a gold-digger and forbid me from ever having anything to do with you again.'

She exhaled on a sigh, shrugging.

'So I took the easy route. I kept Jason my secret, because I knew he was yours and I had loved our time on Crete and I would always have Jason to remind me of those days.'

He stared at her, dark eyes direct and purposeful, 'You're no coward, Alexandra. I have never met a stronger woman.'

She brushed off his comment. 'Hardly strong. I became more of a coward as Jason grew. I wanted you to know about him but I was so scared you'd take him away from me.' She looked up at him through damp lashes. 'And I was right to be scared.'

'But you're letting him go.'

She nodded reluctantly. 'I don't want to. But it's time. It's only fair you get to share in our child. We both had a hand in making him after all.'

Silence fell in the room as both remained motionless for a time. Finally Nick expelled one long breath and moved across the room to face her, reaching out one hand to her face. 'You see what I mean? I've never met a woman with such inner strength.'

Without thinking her face leant into his warm hand automatically and she accepted the caress.

'Single-handedly you've raised our son, struggling through the years. And now you're going to hand him over.'

A lump formed at the back of her throat that swallowing wouldn't budge. Another day his words would have been an accusation. Today they sounded like something approaching respect. Something had changed, something that suddenly gave her the hope and the courage to continue.

'I was wrong,' she started, her voice faltering. 'I believed I was right not to tell you, but it just made things so much more complicated later on. I'm so sorry, Nick—' She dipped her head as tears threatened to fall, and he wound his arms around her and pulled her into his chest.

He stroked her back while his other hand brushed her cheek, feeling the hint of dampness clinging to her soft skin and her harsh, choppy breath puff in short staccato bursts against his skin.

But she didn't burst into tears, as he'd expected

when he'd brought her to his chest, and he could feel the control she was exerting over herself in every ragged breath. No matter what Alexandra herself thought, she was strong. He was tearing her apart inside with his plans to take Jason back to Greece, and yet still she was holding together.

Even though she was right.

He shoved that thought aside. There was no point thinking of the past. Instead he should concentrate on the future, with his son, back in Greece. Though even that thought didn't give him the rush of warmth he was seeking.

Stavros was gone. Jason would have no uncle to welcome him, no *nonna* or *poppo* to spoil their only grandchild.

If they would have spoiled him.

How would they have reacted? To suddenly discover a long-lost grandchild who'd been living half a world away—surely he could have convinced them?

Just as Stavros hadn't?

So what? Stavros had been lied to. Stavros had believed the woman. He hadn't been able to convince their parents.

Would they have believed Jason was Nick's son? It wasn't as if he was a baby any more, where there might have been doubt, surely they would have seen the resemblance.

The emotions of that time came swirling back—the acrimony, the accusations, the harsh words—all of them ugly, only his brother's faith and insistence a bright, though ill-founded light.

And the implicit logic in her words struck home.

They hadn't believed that other child was Stavros's. Why would they have believed Jason was Nick's?

Suddenly the harsh-edged plate that had been lurching inside him cut loose, clattering away and finally clearing his view of history, revealing the truth of her words.

His parents would have been devastated. A replay of the tragedy of their first son's death would have destroyed them. They would never have allowed Alexandra into the family in the wake of what had transpired. She would never have stood a chance.

Even if Nick had believed her.

His gut squeezed even as he sucked in a breath.

There should be no question he would have believed her. He had loved her then. How could he not have believed her?

Though in the atmosphere of that time...

He looked down at the woman in his arms, felt her warm breath through the fine weave of his shirt, absorbed the press of her breasts into his chest and breathed in her fresh woman's scent. He dipped his head, kissing the top of her head.

'It's no wonder you acted as you did,' he said softly. 'You have no need to apologise.'

He felt her reaction like a twitch to start with. She stirred in his arms, lifting her head a fraction, stretchng her arms and unfurling from his chest like a but-terfly making its first tentative moves out of the chrysalis.

Slowly she turned her face up to meet his. She sniffed back one last gulp of air, blinked her questioning eyes clear of moisture and stared up at him.

'Do you mean that?' she asked, almost as if she was afraid she'd misunderstood.

Even with her hair mussed from their contact, the salty tracks on her cheeks evidence of her tears and her lips slightly parted, she'd never looked more beautiful. So strong and yet so vulnerable.

A base primal need to take this woman, to possess her and claim her for ever, overwhelmed him, and a deep, guttural groan that said all of those things welled up from inside—only to be cut off when his lips meshed with hers.

Gently, tenderly, his mouth moved over hers, answering her question the best way he could, trying to obliterate the pain of these last years, attempting to ease all the hurt and anguish she'd suffered at the hands of his family.

Tentatively at first her mouth started to move under his, responding with a gentle pressure of her own until on a sigh her lips parted, welcoming him inside.

Any sense of time was lost as he accepted her invitation, her taste in his mouth fuelling his passion, increasing the intensity of both what he was experiencing and what he was giving. And now he wasn't just trying to ease her pain. Now he was seeking his own absolution.

As if aware of his needs, she kissed his mouth, his lips, his face and eyes, her lips simultaneously soothing yet inflaming wherever they made contact. Her body pressed against his in a way that left no doubt as to where her skin dipped and curved, the sweet concave arc of her waist and the delicious flare of her hips. His hands traced the lines, sculpting her to him as he pressed her even closer.

She would be in no doubt as to his arousal. It was there, pushing out to her even as she seemed to press into its bulge. Her hands scrabbled with his shirt, freeing the fabric from his jeans so that her hands could roam the skin of his back, holding him so firmly he could feel the press of her nails into his skin.

He groaned with the pleasure and the pain and the frustration of the barrier of their clothes. Now his need had grown into something far more insistent, something far more carnal, and skin was what he too needed. The highly charged encounter of skin against skin.

His hands traced behind her, down the slinky fabric of her tiered skirt. Bunching the fabric in his thumbs, he drew the sides of the skirt up, sliding his hands up the backs of her legs as they rose. She gasped in his mouth, shifting her weight so that her legs parted slightly, allowing him access to direct his touch between her legs, up to where they met, her stretch lace panties the only remaining barrier. Her *damp* stretch lace panties. He groaned.

She was fire in his hands, liquid fire, setting him alight with her touch and her taste and her smell, setting his senses reeling and his internal thermostat out of orbit. And she was as aroused as he was. Knowing that threatened to send him off the scale.

Her hands dropped, her fingers inside his belt tugging, insistent.

He took her chin in his hand, forcing her to look up at him. 'Jason?' he asked.

'He'll be gone hours,' she replied, her breath choppy, her eyes dilated and almost luminous in their intensity.

He kissed her then, knowing she'd just answered his unspoken question in the affirmative as her hands continued to scrabble with his belt, forcing their way in to work at the buckle. He leaned over, to give her more room. He ached to be freed, and every time her hands brushed over him, even through the stout denim, her movements drove him crazy.

Now he had better access behind her. His hand slid under the fabric of her panties and he held the goose-bumped flesh of one round cheek of her bottom in one hand. She quivered against him, and hurried her actions. Then his buckle was gone and she worked at the zip, easing the catch over the distended fabric.

He slid his hand down, into the cleft between her legs, into the moist, hot place there. When he slid first one and then two fingers inside her she moaned, her back arching as her breath came fast and urgent.

Almost frantically she pulled aside his jeans and put one palm to the semi-released hardness beneath as the other eased the band of his underwear over. And then he was freed and it was his turn to gasp, her hands searing his skin and inflaming his senses.

Suddenly it wasn't enough for his fingers to be there; he needed to be inside her—all of him. He wrenched down her panties and lifted her skirt away, so that he could feel the spring of her curls against the base of his erection as it pressed into her belly. And he moved her back, bracing her against the wall.

She wound her arms around his neck tightly for support as he lifted her, wrapping her legs around him. One hand braced on the wall, with the other he found her, ready for him, and he placed the tip at her opening.

She cried out something, the words indiscernible, but they spoke to him of her need, her desires, her passion, and he knew that his own matched all of those. He entered her with one long thrust that had her throw back her head against the wall, her eyes wide, her mouth open in shock and delight.

He pulled back, waited on the brink, and thrust again, deeper this time, beads of sweat stinging his eyes and compounding the pain-ecstasy mix. Then faster. She bucked her hips against him, as much as she could in her position, matching every thrust with a tilt of her hips to welcome him, to guide him deeper inside her, into that place where the past would be eradicated, where hurt and blame would be wiped away for ever.

Again and again he withdrew, only to slam into her. Each time the need inside him was building, a hot and urgent thing, unavoidable, unstoppable. She peaked under his onslaught and cried out, the tremors inside her clenching him tightly and forcing his own climax, pumping in his own shattering release.

They huddled together as their shaking subsided, their bodies humming, their breath recovering, her legs finally sliding down to the ground. Her knees buckled and he steadied her, nuzzled the area just below her ear. She tasted salty and warm, the damp tendrils of her hair tickling his nose.

She stood there, her back still pressed against the wall, her arms around his neck, feeling her heartbeat calm as his breath steadied against her hair. She'd thought last week's lovemaking could not be bettered, but this time she was shattered, mentally and physically. And still she wanted him again.

Even as some sense of normality returned to her body, the hunger was there, the need to be close to him, to enclose him in her body.

He'd said she was strong. How wrong could he be? She was lost in his arms, knowing the pleasures to be found there. There was no earthly way she could deny herself those sensations.

Not when she loved him. And he must feel something for her, surely? He'd said she didn't have to apologise, but they hadn't taken the time for him to explain. Were his views softening towards her? Maybe now he would take the opportunity to expand on his words. Maybe now that they had satisfied their physical selves there would be time to talk.

As if sensing her mood, he sighed sharply, his breath a warm blast against her neck, but then he raised his head and pounded one solid fist into the wall. She flinched at the sudden action, at the dull boom just above her head.

'I must be mad.' He wheeled away, zipping up his jeans.

Alexandra stood stock still for a moment, chilled at both the sudden rush of cold where his body had just been and at his words. Her panties lay on the floor in front of her, unmistakable evidence of her folly. She pushed herself shakily off the wall, snatched up the offending article and started for her room. 'If you're mad, then I guess that makes me just plain stupid.'

She ran from the room, waiting for the prickle of tears, but there was none. Instead it was white-hot anger that infused her veins.

He caught up with her in the hall, his hand on the wrist holding her panties, spinning her around.

His eyes looked wild and tortured. 'Maybe we were both stupid. But I'm talking about not using protection. I'm sorry, Alexandra. That's never happened to me before.'

'You're worried I could get pregnant?' She thought

the idea over. It was probably too late in her cycle— her period was due in a day or so—but there was always the chance. The possibility brought a brief smile to her face. To be made pregnant by the same man who was now taking their first child away—it was almost too ironic.

'That's not the only concern. There are other risks too.'

'Well, if it's any consolation,' she said, looking down at his hand on her arm, 'there's no chance you'll catch anything from me. I can assure you of that.'

'Even if I was concerned, how can you be so sure?'

'Because there's never been anyone else, Nick. You've been the only one.' She raised an eyebrow. 'Can you say the same thing?'

He dropped her wrist. 'I'm a man. What do you think?'

Her chin kicked up a notch. 'Oh, I think you're a man.' She purposely misinterpreted his question. 'Didn't you just prove it? But there's probably no need to worry. So don't. I'll let you know if there's a problem—and I *will* let you know.'

'I can't go back to Greece and leave you here— not knowing—like this.'

'I'll be okay, Nick. I'll probably have my period before you get on the plane.' She shrugged. 'Simple as that—problem solved.'

'No. You should come with us. Back to Greece.'

She rubbed her forehead with one hand and stepped

into her room. She couldn't face him like this, naked under her skirt. By the time he'd followed her in she had slipped back into her panties. Somehow it made her feel she was more in control.

'Back to Greece? Why should I do that on the off-chance I could be pregnant? I can't just traipse off to Greece on a whim. I have a life here. Responsibilities. My parents are coming for Christmas—how can I just abandon them? It will be hard enough explaining why Jason has gone—how can I just take off too? Have you just changed your mind about me coming over so that I can look after Jason for those times you won't be there? Or maybe you just like having your sex on tap. Let's face it, I fall so easily into your bed lately—not that I can pretend I don't enjoy it—there's bound to be a bit of sex on the side in it for you.'

He hesitated a fraction, and Alex would just about have sworn she could see the machinations taking place in his mind.

'So marry me,' he said at last. 'Come as my wife!'

CHAPTER TWELVE

'Is THAT a proposal?' She shook her head, disbelieving.

After everything that had happened the idea was too ridiculous. Everything he had done to date suggested he wanted to get as far away as possible from her. He didn't want her to come to Greece to look after Jason and it was patently clear he didn't really want her for his wife.

All this because of the minuscule chance she could be pregnant? Did he still not trust her to the extent that he would marry her rather than risk her hiding another secret pregnancy?

Hadn't he learnt anything?

'It makes perfect sense,' he said, as if his mind was made up. 'You will come to Greece with us. It solves all our problems. We will marry, either here or in Greece. It makes no difference to me.'

'As it makes no difference to me where we will *not* marry.'

'You are refusing to marry me? You surprise me. You would have security—our child, our *children* would be provided for. Isn't that what you want?'

Security. She laughed. Financially she'd be secure, sure. But her heart? How could that ever feel secure, knowing his was lost to her for ever? 'No, Nick. I don't want that.'

'Then what?'

'It's ironic, but the only thing I want from you is the one thing you're incapable of giving.' She paused, picked up the photo of the three of them the stranger had taken that day at the zoo, all smiling, looking for all the world like the happiest family on earth—and it was all a fraud.

She put the photo back down onto the dressing table and sighed. That family didn't exist—couldn't exist—in the vacuum that was his heart.

'I love you, Nick. And all I ask is that you love me in return.' She looked up into the swirling depths of his eyes, saw the tangle of emotions at play, and knew the answer she wanted wasn't there.

'Alexandra...I admit I underestimated you. You're a good mother. I have a lot of respect for you.'

'But you don't love me. You don't trust me. At times I think you even hate me. I can't think why you want to marry me—unless it's to keep me so close there would be no chance I could take Jason away from you again.'

Nick's face hardened and grew dark. 'Then don't come!' His voice boomed in the small room. 'I will take Jason to Greece and you will stay here alone. Alone and bitter. Maybe then you will appreciate—'

There was a movement behind Nick, at the door— a sound—a *cry*. A glimpse of a face, crumpled and agonised, and then he was gone.

'Jason!' Alex shouted as she burst past Nick and out of the room. He was already powering through the front door, his legs like pistons, and his sobs tore at her heart as she tried to catch up.

How much had he heard, standing by the doorway? She had love—her son's love—and pride was going to lose it for her. Stupid pride that wouldn't allow her to be with her son just because his father didn't love her. What the hell was wrong with her?

Over the front verandah he flew, across the patch of front garden and past the car waiting in the driveway. Matt's father's car—they were back early.

'Jason! Stop!'

Out of the corner of her eye she saw Matt's father step out of the car, the question on his face, but there was no time to acknowledge him, no time to explain what was wrong, as Jason sprinted away down the footpath. Behind her the screen door slammed. Nick had joined the chase.

She was gaining. He could outrun her in the end, but for now she was gaining ground, despite her slip-ons flapping, threatening to trip her up at each step.

Her lungs were choked, her heart beating loud in her ears, beating time with the thunder of the two motorbikes accelerating down the street. He looked back at her. She saw his face contorted, eyes squeezed in pain and chin back, as he tried to focus through the tears, and then he turned, blundering on past a parked car and dashing for the road.

'Jason, no!'

There was nothing she could do.

He was so small. So small and so fast they'd never see him in time. Never expect a child to run out from behind the car. Never have time to stop, not this close.

But they might see her. She cut across the footpath and stepped onto the road.

'Noooooo!'

Nick's cry melded with the roar of the machines, the roar that became a storm as the black-leathered riders thundered closer—so close that she could see the panic hit their faces when they saw her on the side of the road, when they saw Jason frozen in fear directly in their path and when their reactions finally allowed them to attempt to stop.

It all happened so quickly. One bike snaked wildly as its rider battled to reign in the whining machine, finally coming to a screeching, smoking halt just inches from the white-faced boy. The other locked its front wheel, sliding out so both rider and machine screamed a path of destruction along the asphalt, tearing and scraping and mangling, and finally collecting the woman who had chosen to run the wrong way.

Not slow motion. *Slow terror.*

The slow, agonising terror of not knowing whether the woman who lay so still and lifeless on the ground was alive or dead. The terror of thinking…

He raced to her side. She looked like a doll—a beautiful sleeping doll, until he got closer and saw the blood pooling onto the road below her head and the leg buckled back on itself beneath her.

Nearby someone groaned and swore—the biker—and Jason, at last able to move, threw himself down next to his mother. Nick gathered the shaking boy into his arms and held on tight as running footsteps sounded behind him.

He touched the fingers of his free hand to her motionless white throat, desperately searching for a pulse. *She had to be alive.*

'Call an ambulance!' he yelled.

He hated hospitals. Hated their antiseptic smell, their long straight corridors, their stark, clinical quality. Hated the way that tucked deep down in the basement would be the morgue, that secret place where they hid the non-living, away where you couldn't see them—unless it was your job to identify them.

Hospitals meant death.

Just stepping inside had made his gut clench in equal measures of revulsion and panic, and only the small, trembling hand he held had stopped him from turning around and walking straight out again. That, and the woman who lay somewhere behind closed doors. The woman who had risked her own life to save that of her son—*their son.*

The woman he loved.

But was it too late?

Anguish welled up inside him. She couldn't die—

not now—not when there was so much he had to make up for.

On the vinyl chair beside him in the cold, bare box that was the waiting room his son sobbed quietly. He undid the damp knot of their hands and wrapped his arm around the boy, nestling him in against his chest. Jason sniffed and swiped his nose with the back of his wrist. Nick pulled a handkerchief from his pocket and passed it to him.

'Do you think…? I mean, what happens if…?' Nick squeezed his son closer as he blew his nose. 'Is Mum going to die?'

Something deep inside Nick that had already been stretched to breaking point fractured as his son gave voice to the question that was his own greatest fear.

'No.' His voice was a bare croak.

'How do you know?' He lifted his tear-stained face and Nick's heart nearly broke at the hope he saw flickering in his eyes—hope he wished with all his soul wasn't false.

'Because we won't let her.'

The boy studied his face, as if judging whether he should believe him, then he blinked and sniffed again and looked back into his lap.

'It's all my fault.'

'No. Don't think that.'

'But if I hadn't run—'

'No,' said Nick, firmer this time. 'It's my fault. I was angry and said some stupid things to your mother. Stupid things I didn't mean. That's why you ran, isn't it?'

The voice, when it came, was so thin and frail it sounded as if it would snap. 'I don't want Mum to be alone.'

Nick cursed inwardly. How much damage had he done? And how could he make it right?

'Neither do I,' he said at last, promising himself he'd do everything in his power to ensure she'd never be alone. Whatever it took, he'd make things right. 'Neither do I.'

Heels clacked on the tile floor and the two of them looked up in the same instant. 'Tilly!' yelled Jason, jumping out of his chair and barrelling down the corridor. 'Aunt Tilly.' He buried his face in her jacket as she hugged him close. The smile she directed to Nick was thin and strained.

'I came as fast as I could. Any word?'

Nick stood, shaking his head and raking hands through his hair. 'Nothing. She was still unconscious when she came in. All we know for sure is she's got a broken leg. They're doing a brain scan and X-rays—checking for internal injuries.'

And it was taking for ever. Someone must know something. Why the hell couldn't they tell them?

As if on cue a middle-aged man wearing scrubs pushed his way through the swing doors and looked around at them, his gaze settling finally on Nick.

'You came in with Alexandra Hammond?'

'That's right.' They all gathered close around the doctor. 'How is she?'

'Well, Mr Hammond, your wife is one very lucky woman.'

Collectively Nick and Tilly sighed their relief, expelling the breath they'd been holding.

'She's going to be okay, then?' Tilly asked.

'She's sustained multiple fractures to her right tibia,' the doctor continued, smiling at their relieved faces, 'and she needed a few stitches to patch up that cut to her head. But other than that we can't find anything too wrong with her. And you'll be very happy to know she's regained consciousness—though she's going to have a bit of a headache for a while.'

'Can we see her?' asked Nick.

'Well, we'll be prepping her for Theatre to set that leg, but I think a five-minute visit will be in order.'

Jason gazed up at the doctor, a perplexed look on his face. 'Excuse me?'

The doctor looked down at the child. 'Yes, son. What is it?'

'He's not called Mr Hammond. His name is Nick Santos.'

The doctor looked back at Nick, confused. 'You're not next of kin?'

'Not *officially*,' he said.

'He's my father,' offered Jason.

'He's family,' said Tilly, nodding.

Nick smiled, hoping for the best. 'Now I just have to convince her.'

* * *

She lay in the bed, bruised and battered, her eyes closed and her slumbering body attached to an array of equipment, beeping and flashing. Nick stood stock still, his progress arrested at the door as he watched their son edge slowly towards the bed. Ashen-faced, he crept up to his mother's side, leaned over and kissed her gently on the cheek.

'I love you, Mum.'

Everyone in the room seemed to hold their breath until Alex's eyelids finally fluttered open, and though her blue eyes were dull with painkillers and shock the wan smile she returned was real enough. 'Jason.' She lifted a hand to reach him. 'I love you, too.'

Tilly moved closer. 'Hey, sis. Don't you know it's dangerous, fooling around with motorbikes?' She planted a gentle kiss on the unblemished side of her sister's bruised forehead. 'Gee, you had us worried there for a while.'

'The Simpson boy—is he okay?' Alex's voice was whisper soft. 'I feel so bad…'

'Don't feel bad,' said the doctor, finally following the party into the room and rechecking all the equipment. 'His leathers saved him from any serious damage. And from what I've heard, right now I suspect he and his brother are more worried about what the police will have to say. Now, if everyone would like to excuse us, I think it's time we were getting Alex over to Theatre to fix that leg.'

Nick cursed softly under his breath, but already the doctor had a hand under Tilly's elbow, ushering both her and Jason towards the door. The doctor then made a move to remove Nick likewise.

'No,' he said firmly, but softly enough not to alarm Alex. 'I must have just one minute alone with her.'

The doctor hesitated.

'It's important.'

'Very well,' the doctor conceded with a brief nod. 'Just one minute.' He moved back to the bed. 'Alex, it seems your *Mr Hammond* wants to have a quick word with you.'

Nick moved to the side of the bed and sat down on the edge, picking up Alex's hand and holding it gently within his own, so as not to disturb the canula taped into the vein.

'Oh, Nick,' she said, finally opening her eyes. 'It's you. I thought my father must be here.'

It was an acknowledgement. Not a greeting. Not a welcome. She was protecting herself, and it stung that she would need to. But it was no wonder. After the way he'd treated her, he didn't deserve more.

Then a tiny wrinkle appeared between her brows. 'But why did he call you Mr Hammond?'

A wry smile came to his lips. 'I suspect the good doctor believes I am your husband.'

'Imagine that,' whispered Alex tightly, turning her head away.

'I'm imagining,' said Nick, drawing her chin gently back to face his. 'And I'm hoping.'

'You are? Even after me turning you down before?' She hesitated, biting her lip. 'I keep thinking this is all my fault. If I'd agreed to marry you then the life of our son would not have been threatened—none of this would have happened.'

He shrugged. 'You could have said yes then. But whatever has happened I would much prefer you to say yes now.'

'After all this—how can you say that?'

'Because now, unlike before, when I demanded that you marry me, now I would like to *ask* you, not tell you what to do. So you can decide for yourself. And so we can give Jason a real family, with a mother and a father who love each other.'

Alex's eyelids flickered. 'But...but that would mean...'

'Exactly.' He smiled and touched her face with his fingers, stroking her skin so that she leant into his gesture.

'I love you, Alexandra. The bitterness I felt at losing my family wouldn't let me see that until now. I had no way of realising just how much I loved you until I'd nearly lost you. And now I know I cannot live without you, without your love. Please don't make me.'

He dropped down suddenly beside the bed, onto one knee. 'Alexandra Hammond, my love, my destiny, will you marry me?'

Misty tears filmed her eyes as the impact of his words hit home.

'Yes,' she whispered. 'Yes, of course I will marry you.'

His lips curled up, almost in grateful thanks, and he kissed her then, so gently and so sweetly, but with such innate power and emotion that a tear squeezed from her eye as her soul recognised that this was right, that the two of them belonged together and their love was for ever.

EPILOGUE

'CATCH me, Dad!' Jason screamed with laughter as he ran along the stony shore, Nick in hot pursuit, as the sun shone down on them from the limitless Aegean sky. It was a perfect Cretan early spring day, the weather fine, with the promise of rain coming later.

Alex watched from her recliner chair, laughing along with them as Nick made unsuccessful dive after dive for his son. It was so good to watch them play together.

But her happiness went deeper than that. Watching the two of them, the two loves of her life, she knew that things could not have turned out better—for all of them.

Jason loved Nick; that was so clear. It was as if his every dream had come true. She thought back to her wedding day, after the ceremony, when Jason had asked Nick if he could call him Dad. Nick had shaken his hand solemnly and thanked him, and told him he could never have received a better wedding present. Then he'd hugged him tightly and she'd seen the sheen blur his eyes even as he'd blinked it away.

As she blinked it away now, laughing again as Nick made one last rush, collecting a screaming Jason up over his head and declaring himself the victor. Jason giggled and squirmed in his arms before being tossed over Nick's shoulder and escaping to the shore to look for treasure from the sea.

Nick ran up puffing to her side, his glossy olive skin rising and falling in a way that held her mesmerised.

Even after being married for two months she was still struck by the beauty of the man, his sheer masculine form, that always brought a rush of blood and lust through her veins.

She shifted position slightly, noticing his own appreciative gaze on her. He made her feel so beautiful, so incredibly sexy, merely with a glance or a smile.

He squatted down alongside her and kissed her, one hand caressing her once damaged leg, sending sparks through her skin.

'Is your leg all right? Can I get you anything?'

She smiled back at him. He was so concerned for her welfare. She wasn't used to having someone look after her, and she felt spoilt and special and very, very loved. And while he'd been disappointed at first that she hadn't become pregnant that time, before they were married, it had given the three of them a special time to bond together as a family at last.

'I'm fine—just being lazy. I was thinking about Christmas. There was something special about having Tilly and my parents over for our wedding, and for a real Greek Christmas. A double celebration. I know we all enjoyed it. Thank you for making all that possible.'

'You've already thanked me, Alexandra. Not that you need to—I think families are the most important thing, and I don't think I would appreciate that as much if I hadn't lost almost everything.'

'I'm glad Sofia could join us. She looks so much happier now. Do you think she and Dimitri will marry?'

Nick raised his eyebrows. 'I don't know. Though I think she's realised herself that she needs time to get over her father's death before she commits to any one man.'

He traced the back of one finger down the side of her face and she drew in breath, smiling as she realised he would always have this effect on her. He would always be able to move her soul and rock her emotions, just with one touch, one word.

'It's lovely to see you smile,' he said. 'To see you smile without worries. In the last few weeks, even in the last few days, you have looked more beautiful than ever.'

His words fired her heart, tugged at her senses. Would she never get used to the impact he made on her?

'That's because I'm so happy. Happy to be with you. And happy to be back here again. Thank you for deciding on Crete for this holiday.'

'Where else could we go? This is where we began.'

She smiled. 'Back where it all started. Back where Jason began.'

His eyes flared. 'That thought had crossed my mind. Do you suspect you might be more fertile in Crete?'

She knew what he had in mind, and the sparks he had generated inside her moved up to a slow burn. 'I don't know, but it's a good theory.'

He picked up her hand and kissed it softly, looking up at her through his dark lashes.

'A theory I intend to test thoroughly.'

She moistened her lips, knowing just what was in store and looking forward to it as his lips descended purposefully towards hers.

She wrapped her arms around his neck and pulled him closer.

'I was hoping you might say that.'

The world's bestselling romance series.

HARLEQUIN®
Presents

Seduction and Passion Guaranteed!

FROM BOARDROOM TO BEDROOM

**Harlequin Presents® brings you two
original stories guaranteed to make
your Valentine's Day extra special!**

THE BOSS'S MARRIAGE ARRANGEMENT
by *Penny Jordan*

Pretending to be her boss's mistress is one thing—but now
everyone in the office thinks Harriet is Matthew Cole's
fiancée! Harriet has to keep reminding herself it's all just
for convenience, but how far is Matthew prepared to go
with the arrangement—marriage?

HIS DARLING VALENTINE
by *Carole Mortimer*

It's Valentine's Day, but Tazzy Darling doesn't care.
Until a secret admirer starts bombarding her with gifts!
Any woman would be delighted—but not Tazzy. There's
only one man she wants to be sending her love tokens, and
that's her boss, Ross Valentine. And her secret admirer
couldn't possibly be Ross...could it?

The way to a man's heart...is through the bedroom

SPOTLIGHT

Every month we'll spotlight original stories from Harlequin and Silhouette Books' Shining Stars!

Fantastic authors, including:

- Debra Webb
- Julie Elizabeth Leto
- Merline Lovelace
- Rhonda Nelson

Plus, value-added Bonus Features are coming soon to a book near you!

- Author Interviews
- Bonus Reads
- The Writing Life
- Character Profiles

SIGNATURE SELECT SPOTLIGHT
On sale January 2005

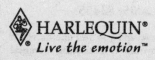

HARLEQUIN®
Live the emotion™

Silhouette®
Where love comes alive™

The world's bestselling romance series.

HARLEQUIN®
Presents

Seduction and Passion Guaranteed!

GREEK
TYCOONS

They're the men who have everything—except a bride....

Wealth, power, charm—what else could a heart-stoppingly
handsome tycoon need? In the GREEK TYCOONS
miniseries you have already been introduced to some
gorgeous Greek multimillionaires who are in need of wives.

THE GREEK BOSS'S DEMAND
by *Trish Morey*
On sale January 2005, #2444

THE GREEK TYCOON'S
CONVENIENT MISTRESS
by *Lynne Graham*
On sale February 2005, #2445

THE GREEK'S
SEVEN-DAY SEDUCTION
by *Susan Stephens*
On sale March 2005, #2455

Pick up a Harlequin Presents® novel and you will enter a world
of spine-tingling passion and provocative, tantalizing romance!

Available wherever Harlequin books are sold.

www.eHarlequin.com

The world's bestselling romance series.

Seduction and Passion Guaranteed!

Looking for stories that sizzle?

Wanting a read that has a little extra spice?

Harlequin Presents® is thrilled to bring you romances that turn up the heat!

Don't miss...

AT THE SPANISH DUKE'S COMMAND

by bestselling MIRA® author

Fiona Hood-Stewart

On sale February 2005, #2448

Pick up a PRESENTS PASSION™ novel— where seduction is guaranteed!

Available wherever Harlequin books are sold.

The world's bestselling romance series.

HARLEQUIN®
Presents

Seduction and Passion Guaranteed!

Back by popular demand...

EXPECTING!

She's sexy, successful and PREGNANT!

Relax and enjoy our fabulous series about
couples whose passion results in pregnancies...
sometimes unexpected!

Share the surprises, emotions, drama and suspense
as our parents-to-be come to terms with the prospect
of bringing a new life into the world. All will
discover that the business of making babies brings
with it the most special love of all....

Our next arrival will be

HIS PREGNANCY BARGAIN by *Kim Lawrence*
On sale January 2005, #2441
Don't miss it!

THE BRABANTI BABY by *Catherine Spencer*
On sale February 2005, #2450